The Garden of My Imaan

For Apa
and
for my mother

With grateful thanks to Jennifer Unter, Kathy Landwehr, and Vicky Holifield

Published by
PEACHTREE PUBLISHERS
1700 Chattahoochee Avenue
Atlanta, Georgia 30318-2112
www.peachtree-online.com

Text © 2013 by Farhana Zia

First trade paperback edition published in 2016

Cover design by Maureen Withee
Book design and composition by Melanie McMahon Ives

Printed in the United States of America in January 2016 by RR Donnelley & Sons in Harrisonburg, VA
10 9 8 7 6 5 4 3 2 (hardcover)
10 9 8 7 6 5 4 3 2 1 (trade paperback)

Library of Congress Cataloging-in-Publication Data

Zia, F. (Farhana)
  The garden of my Imaan / Farhana Zia.
    p. cm.
  Summary: The arrival of new student Marwa, a fellow fifth-grader who is a strict Muslim, helps Aliya come to terms with her own lukewarm practice of the faith and her embarrassment over others' reactions to their beliefs.
    ISBN 978-1-56145-698-7 (hardcover) / 978-1-56145-921-6 (trade paperback)
    [1. Self-acceptance—Fiction. 2. Muslims—Fiction. 3. Islam—Customs and practices—Fiction. 4. Schools—Fiction. 5. East Indian Americans—Fiction. 6. Family life—Fiction. 7. Toleration—Fiction. 8. Family life—Fiction.] I. Title.
      PZ7.Z482Gar 2013
  [Fic]—dc23

                          2012028138

FARHANA ZIA

PEACHTREE
ATLANTA

A little girl threw a mango seed in dry, pebbly soil and walked away. "I will grow a mango tree," she announced.

"If you want the fruit," her mother said, "you must tend the seed."

So the girl went back. First she tilled the soil. Then she dug a hole and covered the seed with earth. She watered it every day and labored to keep the ground free of weeds and pests. One day a seedling poked its little head out. The girl planted pretty flowers around the sapling. Soon they blossomed and their perfume filled the air. Butterflies, birds, and bees came to nest and the garden grew and grew.

When the girl became a woman, she held her own daughter on her lap. "A garden bloomed in dry soil," she told her. "It was a garden of imaan."

"Imaan?" her daughter asked.

"It's our belief," the woman explained. "The seed lies, oh so quietly within, until one day it grows into a sprout and the sprout into a sapling and the sapling into a tree and the bud arrives next to uncurl one pretty petal at a time."

"And the mango? Tell me about the mango," the daughter begged.

The woman laughed. "Oh, it grew," she said. "And it was so soft and sweet, the golden juice dribbled like a golden river from arm to elbow!"

Badi Amma told this story to Amma, who told it to me.

Driving Camels

There is a lake not far from my house, with a sandy beach on one end and spongy walking trails on the other. In the summer, Zayd and I go there to swim and *Amma*, our grandmother, tags along. When *Badi Amma* was stronger, she'd come too. Our great-grandmother loved to kick up the sand with her toes.

Our little beach is just about the only sandy place we have close by. As far as I know, there are no deserts to speak of in the Northeast, only mountains to the west, the ocean to the east, and a coastal plain in between. I remember all this because I made a travel brochure in fourth grade social studies class one year ago.

And so, when the crazy lady screamed at us about deserts, I didn't know what she was talking about, but she pretty much ruined our day.

That morning, Mom was really annoyed that I didn't get out of bed when she called me, but a storm had kept me tossing and turning for most of the night and it was hard to wake up. Fifteen minutes later, I heard her arguing with Zayd too. By 9:30, we were on the road to Sunday school. By 9:45, we were stuck in traffic, still some distance away from the intersection where we normally turned left to go to the Islamic Center of Wilshire County.

"Sister Khan's going to be mad," I muttered. My Sunday school teacher already had a pretty bleak opinion of me. I had missed two classes so far. I didn't know the verses of the holy Quran as well as my friends did. And worst of all, I didn't fast on weekdays during the holy month of *Ramadan,* even though, according to her, I was old enough and sound of body and mind.

"We could've left the house a lot earlier if you'd gotten out of bed sooner," Mom reminded me.

"Sundays should be for rest," I grumbled. "Saturdays are taken up with soccer practice and math tutoring and weekdays are reserved for school. When do I ever get to rest?"

A car honked behind us and then several others followed its lead.

"Looks like the lights aren't working right." Mom craned her neck to see ahead of us. "Maybe the wind knocked the wires down last night."

"There should be someone directing traffic," I said. "Where's the cop?"

"Sleeping in on Sunday," my brother Zayd chimed in.

"We're going to be really late." I kept an eye on the dashboard clock, already trying to prepare myself for Sister

Khan's comments about punctuality and tardiness.

We inched our way forward and finally came to the intersection where the traffic light flashed red. Mom hesitated, waiting to see if someone would let us through.

I saw an opening in the oncoming traffic and yelled, "Go, Mom!"

She stepped on the gas and whipped the car into a left turn.

"Watch out!" I shouted. Our tires squealed as she shot into the intersection, toward a car that had appeared out of nowhere. Mom slammed on the brakes and we came to a jerky stop, narrowly avoiding a collision. The other car swerved around us.

"Do you want to kill someone?" the driver screamed out her window. "Go back to the desert, moron! Drive a camel!"

I could see her glaring angrily at us as she sped away.

Flustered, Mom tugged at her dupatta, which had started to slide off her head. "Sorry," she muttered to herself. "It was a stupid mistake."

Quietly, I eased my own scarf off my head.

My brother poked me on the shoulder. "What did she mean, 'Go back to the desert'? We're not from the desert, are we?"

"Just shut up, Zayd!" I snapped.

"And what did she mean, 'drive a camel'?" he persisted. "No one drives camels. They ride them, don't they?"

"Ignorant woman!" Mom shook her head. "She thinks we're Arabs."

"It was the hijab, wasn't it?" I asked.

Mom noticed me playing with my scarf in my lap. "What are you doing?"

"Nothing… I'll put it back on in a sec."

"Oh, Aliya!" Mom sounded exasperated.

Zayd piped up from the backseat. "Hey, Mom, did you ever do that?"

"Do what, Zayd?"

"Ride a camel?"

"No!" Mom said sharply.

"Did Amma or Badi Amma?"

Mom sighed and moved forward another car length. "Of course not, Zayd. Why would they do that?"

"I don't know," Zayd said. "It would be kind of fun to sit on top of the hump and go bumpity bump."

"There are no camels in India, you idiot," I pointed out.

"There are camels in Rajasthan, but that's very much beside the point," Mom said. "And besides, Rajasthan is one thousand miles from where Amma lived."

"Why would that woman say that, Mom?" I asked.

"Because she's an ignorant person who doesn't know her geography and has no clue about things in general." Mom's brow creased with worry. "She clearly doesn't know that Muslims come from all corners of the world. Just put it entirely out of your mind, okay?"

But that was hard to do. We drove the rest of the way in silence.

Blue-eyed Boyfriend

We were twenty minutes late and I knew I was in for it. Zayd and I sped up the stairs. As he ran toward the younger kids' classroom, I dashed into the door marked Religion 2.

"*Assalam alaikum,*" Sister Khan called out. "Notice, people. We started thirty minutes ago."

"Twenty," I mumbled, making my way to the last row, where my friends Nafees, Sehr, Heba, and Amal sat.

"Reason, please?" asked Sister Khan.

"We were stuck in traffic," I said, sliding into my seat. Under my breath, I added, "That's what happens when you drive a camel."

"What?" Sehr looked confused.

I dug in my backpack for my notebook and pencil. "What's the assignment?"

"She wants a two-page essay on *The Five Essential Practices of Islam and Applications in Our Lives,*" Heba whispered.

"Two pages? Are you serious?" I peeked into Nafees's notebook but she snapped it shut.

"I'm done!" she announced.

"That's not two pages," I said.

"No talking!" Sister Khan called out.

"What are you writing about?" I asked Heba, keeping my voice down.

"Ramadan. What else?"

I chewed on my pencil. I could fill up two pages with Badi Amma's stories about her pilgrimage to Mecca, but I had a feeling Sister Khan might want something about daily prayers or charity instead. I started writing but Nafees was distracting me. She had opened her notebook again and was drawing hearts pierced with arrows and dripping blood. Then she scribbled a quick note, ripped the page out, and tossed it into Sehr's lap.

Sehr read the note and turned to stare at Nafees as if she had just sprouted horns. Amal and Heba read it next and their jaws dropped. I pushed my assignment aside and grabbed the note from Amal.

Guess what? I have a boyfriend! He has blue eyes and he is sooo cuuuute!!! My parents don't know—if you tell, I'll never speak to you again.

I read it four times. Nafees had a boyfriend? She wasn't even supposed to talk to boys! Her family had arrived from Pakistan a year ago and her parents were still trying to figure things out.

Nafees had told us about their shouting matches. "They

forbid dancing and they won't let me download any music," she'd complain. "If I switch on the car radio, they scream their heads off!" Her parents had made her wear hijab as soon as her period started and they were looking into an Islamic school for her as well. How could Nafees have a boyfriend?

But before I could get more details, Sister Khan rapped on her desk and told us to attend to our assignment.

After Religion 2, I had Arabic class, then Quranic reading. I wasn't very good at either, so I did my best to pay attention in class even though I was dying to hear more about Nafees's new boyfriend.

Finally it was time for lunch. We hurried to the social hall, pushing our way through crowds of kids pouring in from their classes.

"Are you going to tell us the rest or not?" I demanded. "We have exactly twenty-five minutes until midday prayers."

Nafees was more than happy to oblige. "His name is Marc, short for Marcus. He has the cutest ponytail."

"Marc?" Amal raised her eyebrows. "That's not even a Muslim name!"

"Your parents are going to have a fit," Heba declared. "How'd you—"

"We met in the grocery store. Isn't that romantic?"

"And?" I wanted to know more.

"And…he was eating potato chips and he said hi and I said hi back and—"

"He was eating *before* he paid for the chips?"

"Shut up, Sehr!" Nafees said.

"How do you do it?" I asked.

"Do what?"

"This." I swept my hand in her direction. "The way you talk to people so easily. The way you make new friends all the time."

I thought about Josh Clemens, the cute kid in Mr. Gallagher's homeroom. His eyes were blue too.

Nafees snapped her fingers in my face. "Like this!" she said. "It's easy."

"You're unbelievable!" I marveled.

"I just don't know about all this." Sehr was frowning. "What happens next?"

Nafees giggled. "I'll keep you posted."

I chewed on my lip, still trying to wrap my brain around what I just heard. "What's the matter with you?" Sehr asked. "You seem sort of—"

"Nothing," I replied quickly, turning back to my lunch. In a year or so, I'd be as old as Nafees and Amal. Maybe Josh would finally notice me and I could get a boyfriend too.

It was almost time for midday prayers, so I stuffed the last bite of my tuna sandwich into my mouth. I felt wildly jealous of Nafees. She had what I'd been wishing for: a real boyfriend. Josh, to be precise. I'd had a serious crush on him since the middle of fourth grade, but we'd barely spoken more than two words to each other.

Amal cleared her throat. "I've got news too."

"What, now you have a boyfriend?" I asked.

"Ha, ha, very funny!"

"We're *waiting*," Sehr prompted.

"Well…it's not as exciting as having a boyfriend, but it's pretty important. I'm starting hijab."

She was right. The news of her decision to start covering herself wasn't as astounding as Nafees's, but it was still surprising. Amal's family was pretty liberal—the exact opposite of Nafees's.

"I don't understand," I said. "Why?"

"Because…you know," she whispered conspiratorially. "I've started my period, that's why."

"Really?" I squealed. "You have? How do you feel? Is it really different?"

Last year, I'd begged Mom to let me wear a bra. "What's the rush?" she'd said, eyeing the rolled-up T-shirt under my top with suspicion. "Your breasts will develop soon enough." I told her that Madison and Carly already had bras, so she gave in and let me get a plain white one. But there was nothing happening on the period front just yet, and there wasn't much I could do about it. Mom told me not to worry. Some girls just took a little longer. But I couldn't help wondering and wishing, especially since my friends were way ahead of me.

"Well, well!" Sehr said with a big smile. "Congratulations, Amal. You're a real woman now!"

"Your parents want you to do this?" I asked.

"They don't…not really," Amal admitted. "But I want to."

"What did your mom say?" Heba asked. "She can't be thrilled."

"She was surprised," Amal admitted. "She asked me if I was very, very sure."

"And are you?" Heba wondered.

"Sure, I'm sure." Amal's voice was strong and confident.

"But aren't you a little bit afraid?" I asked, thinking about the woman who had yelled at us that morning.

"Afraid? Of what?" she asked.

"Of what people might think? Of being teased?"

"No way!" Amal replied. "I'm not afraid to be a Muslim."

"But you can be one without needing to look like one, right?" I asked.

"Why do you worry so much what other people think?" Nafees demanded.

"I don't like to stick out," I said. "I can't help it."

"My older sister's been sticking out for two years without any problems," Sehr said. "She started wearing hijab when she was fourteen."

All this talk about hijab was making me uneasy. I turned to Nafees. "Tell us more about Marc."

"Not today." Nafees winked at me. "I want to keep the rest of him to myself for now."

"Eat up," Heba urged, biting into her Syrian bread and falafel sandwich. "There won't be lunch breaks once Ramadan starts."

We finished our lunch, threw away our trash, and left the social hall.

"Who's excited to fast again this year?" Heba asked on our way to the prayer hall.

"What a silly question!" Amal said. "We all are!"

"I can't wait for Eid," Sehr said enthusiastically.

"Whoa! Let Ramadan start, will you? Let's get through a month of fasting before we get excited about celebrating its end," Nafees said.

"When exactly does Ramadan start, anyway?" I asked.

"The second week in November," Amal said. "How could you not know that?"

"I haven't been thinking about it yet," I replied. "I suppose I'll fast on weekends like last yea— Hey, wait a minute! Isn't Thanksgiving a couple of weeks later?"

Sehr ignored my question. "Only on weekends?" She sounded surprised. "Why?"

"Oh...school," I stammered. "You know..."

"My little sister already fasts on school days and she's only ten," Sehr said.

Nafees pointed at me. "Let me guess. You don't want to fast on school days because you don't want to *stick out*, right? Fraidy cat!"

My cheeks felt hot. There were plenty of other legitimate reasons for not fasting on a school day—reasons that had to do with PE and math and tests and focus and concentration. But I kept my mouth shut. Sehr would probably say my reasons were lame.

"Oh, leave her alone, Nafees," Amal demanded. "Mind your own business!"

"All right!" Nafees said. "No need to be so sensitive."

I mouthed a silent *thank you* to Amal.

"Don't worry about it," Amal said. "We all try to do our best and others should mind their own business." She glared at Nafees.

We didn't talk much after that. Quickly, we made ablutions in the *wudu* room to cleanse ourselves for prayer and removed our shoes before entering the prayer hall.

People were sitting on the floor waiting for midday prayers to begin, men in front and women in the back. The large room wasn't as crowded as it would be on a celebration day like *Eid* and there were a lot of empty rows.

I joined Mom in the back of the room, where she sat chatting quietly with Amal's mother. The women around us wore all sorts of clothing—*abayas, shalvar khameez, saris,* and even jeans. Everyone had their heads covered. Mom's dupatta kept sliding off; while she talked, her fingers fiddled nervously with it.

Zayd and his friends sat in front of us. If *Baba* had been there, Zayd would have had to sit up front with the other men and boys, but our dad was in Detroit for business.

The strange events of the morning had left me feeling uneasy and jittery. But as I waited for the midday prayer to begin, I closed my eyes and took a deep breath. I relaxed all my muscles and tried to let my mind calm down.

At the stroke of one, the call to prayer sounded. The entire congregation stood up and waited for the *Imam* to lead us in worship. *"Allahu Akbar!"* Imam Malik declared. God is great! We bowed, kneeled, and prostrated together according to our tradition, placing our foreheads on the prayer mats in submission to God. We all recited the same words together.

I closed my eyes and added a little extra. *O merciful Allah,* I prayed. *Help me be less of a fraidy cat, please?*

Amma and Badi Amma

Zayd hadn't forgotten the angry woman's words. The next morning, he looked up from his cereal. "Hey Amma, did you sit on top of a camel when you were a little girl?"

"Watch it, Zayd!" I covered up my bowl with both my hands. "Don't talk with your mouth full! Sheesh!"

Badi Amma looked up from her morning tea. "What is this *camel wamel*? Camel rides are only for peasants." Then my great-grandmother turned to me. "And what is this *sheesh weesh*?"

"But Amma," Zayd persisted. "You didn't answer my question."

"No, Zayd," my grandmother replied. "I am sure I have not sat on a camel, but I made many paper boats when I was a child, and I jumped rope too." She gave me a quizzical look, so I told her about the rude woman who yelled at us at the intersection.

Amma shook her head. "People need to take the time to learn about each other," she said.

"It was our scarves that made her say that," I told her.

"People say and do offensive things, Aliya," Amma said. "The thing is, how much of it do we allow to get under our skin?"

"Uh-huh…right." I rolled my eyes.

"No, really. Let's look at the elephant, for example. A dog barks at him, and what does the elephant do? He merely sways his tail, *swish swish*, and moves on. He doesn't bother with the barking dog."

So now I'm an elephant?

"Camel rides! Hunh!" my great-grandmother muttered. "Such a silly notion!"

"You two better hurry up and finish your breakfast or you'll miss the school bus," Amma warned.

"It's okay, Amma." Zayd grinned at her. "You can drive us."

"Oh no I won't, mister!" Amma growled in mock anger.

"By the way," I said. "Did you know Thanksgiving's in Ramadan this year?"

"Hmm, so it is." My grandmother didn't sound the least bit worried.

Zayd's spoon froze midway to his mouth. "What are we going to do?" he asked. Even he could see this was going to be problematic. After all, Ramadan was about fasting and Thanksgiving was about eating.

"We'll fast during the day, and then we'll enjoy our turkey after sunset, that's what we'll do." Amma made it all sound so simple.

"How will you tell if there's enough salt in the mashed potatoes if you can't taste them while you're cooking?" I asked.

"Famous cooks don't have to taste," Amma smiled. "They can sniff and tell the food is just right!"

I ate the last of my cereal. "Is *Choti Dahdi* coming this year?"

Choti Dahdi was Badi Amma's first cousin—my great-grandaunt. She lived in Minnesota but often arrived unexpectedly during holidays, staying for days and days and screeching at me and Zayd when we displeased her in any way.

"We won't know until she pops in, will we?" Amma replied.

Badi Amma hunched so low over her tea, her nose almost dipped into her cup. A coughing fit wracked her withered frame and she almost keeled over.

"*Aap theek hain*?" I asked in alarm. "Are you okay, Badi Amma?"

"*Oonh! Oonh!*" she moaned. "My chest is going *khrrr-khrrr!* Can you hear?"

I rubbed her back. Her bones felt fragile under my palms. My great-grandmother was very old; I worried about her every time she got sick.

Amma hurried over. "You must be catching a cold, Ma."

"You're a very good catcher, Badi Amma." Zayd laughed at his lame joke. "You never drop the cold. You're always catching it!"

"*Kya bole?*" My great-grandmother cupped her hand to her ear. "What did you say?" Sometimes it was a good thing she couldn't hear very well.

Amma's eyes went to the clock. "*Juldi!*" she reminded us. "Hurry up!"

"You worry too much, Amma," Zayd said.

"Come, Zayd," I said, pushing my chair back. "Get a move on!"

"Okay, Aliya!" Zayd shouted.

"Kya bole?" My great-grandmother eyed him with disapproval.

"He called me Aliya, Badi Amma," I said.

My great-grandmother turned to my brother. "Aliya *Apa!*" She put the emphasis on Apa. "She is your older sister, you *budmash* little boy! Do not forget to show respect!"

"I am *not* naughty," Zayd growled. "Am I, Amma?"

"Go, Zayd!" ordered Amma.

"*Khuda Hafiz!*" Badi Amma called as we ran out the door.

"Yes, Khuda Hafiz," said Amma. "May Allah watch over you!"

The door shut behind us with a loud thud, making our *Bismillah* plaque swing on its nail. *In the name of Allah*, it said. That's what Badi Amma always said too—*every good step must be taken in the name of Allah.*

Winnie had beaten us to the bus stop again. As the bus turned the corner, she waved, urging me to run faster. "*Rapido!*" she yelled.

"I'm running as fast as I can, Winnie," I panted. "But what's with the Spanish all of a sudden?"

"I'm practicing. Señora Bell says we'll learn faster if we use it every day."

After we settled in our seats, I told Winnie about the woman who'd yelled at us. "She thought we were from Saudi Arabia or some other Middle Eastern country. It must have been our scarves. Isn't that stupid?"

"Yeah," said Winnie. "Did you yell back at her?"

"No," I admitted. "I was kind of scared by the whole thing. It was totally unexpected."

"I can't believe your mother turned in front of her, though," Winnie said. "She could've gotten you killed, right?"

"She didn't mean to. It was an accident." Winnie obviously didn't get it. This wasn't about Mom.

"Maybe the *loco mujer* didn't mean it either. Maybe she was scared. Your mom could have killed her too."

"Whose side are you on anyway?" I grumbled. "She could have stopped at 'moron'."

"You'd be okay with being called a moron?"

"Oh, let's forget the whole thing." I turned to stare out the window.

"I've never seen you in a scarf. Why were you wearing them anyway?" Winnie asked.

"We always wear them when we go to the Center."

"Weird. Why not at other times?"

"Because Mom feels Muslim women can be modest without covering themselves up all the time and I agree with her completely, that's why," I said. "Why are you asking anyway?"

"You're the one who brought it up," Winnie said.

We rode in silence for a while. Kids got on at every stop and filled the rows in front of us. Leah plopped into the seat across the aisle. "Have you heard?" She popped her gum loudly. "We're getting a new student in fifth grade. A girl."

"It's the middle of October," I remarked. "She's going to have a lot of catching up to do."

"Her teacher's not going to be happy to have an extra kid, I bet," Winnie said.

"Yeah," I said. "Our classes are already pretty crowded."

The bus made a left turn and I saw Austin kicking a soda can down the sidewalk. I scrunched down in my seat. Austin was the biggest bully in our grade and I hoped every day that he'd be sick and have to stay home. "I wonder what he's going to say to me today."

"Don't worry," Winnie said. "I'll stand up for you."

"Thanks, Win," I sighed. "I just wish I wasn't always so nervous around him."

Austin lumbered down the aisle. I sank down further as he approached, but he passed us and sat in the back.

The kid next to him slipped out and stood in the aisle, looking for another place to sit.

"You, back there!" barked the bus driver. "Return to your seat and buckle up immediately!"

The boy sat back down in a hurry and pressed his nose against the window as though he wanted to disappear through it.

"See? It's not just you who's scared of Austin!" Winnie said.

The bus turned into Carly's neighborhood, the last stop before school. "Carly's not there again," I observed.

"She's been out sick for a while," Winnie said. "I hope it's not too serious. We should call her."

"Yeah," I agreed. "Or make her a get-well card."

"Hey," Winnie said, changing the subject. "I forgot to tell you. I heard Juliana's moving."

"What?" It was so loud on the bus that I couldn't be sure I'd heard her right.

"She's going to another school."

"Are you sure?" I couldn't believe it. "How do you know? Are you 100 percent positive?"

"Yeah. She's going someplace called Sky Vale. Must be a private school," Winnie mused. "Her family can afford it. And guess who's going to be pretty sad?"

"Josh?"

"Bingo!" She grinned. "And with Juliana out of the picture, you can finally say hello to him! *Comprendes*?"

The bus pulled into the school driveway and Winnie was halfway down the aisle before I could ask her any more questions.

The Girl in Hijab

Mrs. Holmes met us at the door and signaled me to follow her. Winnie gave me an uh-oh look. Being called into the principal's office usually meant trouble. I wondered what I'd done. But Mrs. Holmes was smiling and that gave me hope.

I trailed behind her through the front room, past the secretary's desk, and into her office. Her desk was cluttered with papers, file folders, and all sorts of pens and highlighters. Both of the visitor's chairs were occupied.

"Aliya, say hello to Marwa Rajab," Mrs. Holmes said. "She'll be joining our Glen Meadow community."

The new girl turned to face me and smiled.

My eyes went straight to her head. In all my years at Glen Meadow, I had never seen anyone in a hijab. There had been other Muslim kids, but none as obvious as this.

The girl's mother got up from her chair. "Assalam alaikum!" she said.

She was a pretty lady, slightly plump. Her round face was framed by a scarf, and her flowing gown reached down to her ankles.

"Um…hi…," I mumbled.

"Very nice meeting you." Mrs. Rajab had a distinct accent, but it didn't sound like Amma's. "You Muslim?"

I nodded, wondering how she knew and why it mattered anyway.

"*Ma'sha Allah!* Marwa Muslim too." She smiled. "Her dad has new job in this town now."

Dumbly, I nodded again. I couldn't think of a thing to say.

"I love the sound of your language." Mrs. Holmes turned to me. "Isn't 'assalam alaikum' Arabic for 'Peace be upon you'?"

"Uh-huh." Although Arabic was *not* my language, I knew some phrases and verses from the Quran by heart. "And Ma'sha Allah means 'Praise be to God.'"

"How nice!" Mrs. Holmes said. "Perhaps we could use this lovely greeting in our morning announcement some time. What do you think of that idea?"

I shrugged. Why would our principal want to use the Islamic greeting at Glen Meadow? "Good morning" worked just fine.

While Mrs. Holmes asked Mrs. Rajab some questions, I sneaked a look at Marwa. She was dressed in dark pants and a flowered shirt. Her skin was very fair. Not a single wisp of hair peeked through the blue scarf framing her face, so I couldn't tell what color it was. She wore round glasses just like Winnie's. Behind the lenses, her hazel eyes followed mine, observing me checking her out. Unlike her mother, she was tall and thin. She held her head high, the way Mom always told me to.

Apparently finished with her questions, Mrs. Holmes looked over at me. "Marwa and her family moved here from Detroit," she said. Then she turned to Marwa. "I'm sure they were sorry to see you go."

"Marwa live Morocco before Michigan," Mrs. Rajab offered. "But soon she be American girl...*Insha' Allah!*"

Insha' Allah! God willing. I could tell that Mrs. Rajab really meant it.

"You be Marwa friend?" she asked me. "You help her feels welcome?"

"Aliya's an old hand here," Mrs. Holmes assured her. "She'll certainly help Marwa settle in."

"Old hand?"

"That means I've been here a pretty long time," I explained.

"Very good," Mrs. Rajab said. "Marwa be old hand soon with you helping her, Insha' Allah?"

I turned to Mrs. Holmes. "Is she going to be in my homeroom?"

The principal shook her head. "She's in Mr. Gallagher's class."

"Oh?" Mrs. Rajab sounded disappointed. "They not in same room?"

"Well, no, but they'll have plenty of opportunities to interact. I asked Aliya here because I...well, because I thought she'd be a good friend to Marwa."

I wished Mrs. Holmes had picked Maggie or Sarah or Tracy. They were in Mr. Gallagher's homeroom. Marwa and I would probably be on entirely different schedules except for lunch and recess.

The principal stood up. "We'd better head on now. It's getting a bit late."

"Okay, good." Mrs. Rajab turned to me as we left the office. "Where you coming from, Aliya?"

Why did people always ask me that? I knew what Mrs. Rajab wanted to know, but I didn't want to answer her. "I'm from here. I'm American."

"I means, where you mother and father coming from, original?"

I couldn't hold back a sigh. I hated having to explain about my family. "They're from here too," I said, hoping I hadn't seemed rude. "At least my dad is. My mom was born in India, but she came here when she was a little girl. My grandmother came from India a very long time ago. My great-grandmother came later and now we all live together."

Mrs. Rajab smiled. "Big, big family living together in Morocco too."

Our principal draped her arm over Marwa's shoulders and walked her down the hallway. I followed like a robot. Kids turned to stare as we passed. My face felt hot. Was I going to be the *other* Muslim girl at Glen Meadow now? Mrs. Holmes's heels clicked on the polished floor and Mrs. Rajab's abbayah fluttered and swished around her heels.

Marwa walked silently beside me. Up close, she wasn't that much taller but she held herself upright like an exclamation point. I straightened my back, pulling out of my usual slouch. I saw Marwa's eyes flicker, but I couldn't tell what she was thinking.

Just before she entered Mr. Gallagher's room, Marwa waved. "Bye," she said softly. "See you at lunch."

"I'm counting on you to be an excellent host, Aliya," Mrs. Holmes reminded me. "Don't let me down!"

"Assalam alaikum," Mrs. Rajab said. "You very good girl to help in this. Thanks you."

I mumbled the Arabic greeting and ducked down the hall quickly, glad to get away.

Juliana's chair was upturned on her desk. I slid into my seat next to Winnie. "I guess she's really moving, huh?" I asked, nodding toward the empty desk.

"That's what I heard," she said.

I held up both fists and gave a silent cheer.

Winnie was my partner on the social studies report, and she had it spread out in front of her. We had a lot of unfinished work ahead of us; if she weren't quite so meticulous, we'd be done by now. "So what happened in Mrs. Holmes's office?" she asked.

I told her all about Marwa. "I don't know why she picked me," I added. "Don't you think Maggie or Sarah would have been a lot better? They're in her homeroom."

"It's probably because you're Muslim like her," Winnie said.

"We're not the same!" I insisted. "She's from Morocco, she speaks Arabic at home, and she wears a hijab."

"You mean the scarf thingamajiggy? You know who'd look super cute in one? Your great-grandmother!"

"No way. No hijabs in my family."

"I know. I know. But if your Buddy Ma wore a hijab thingy, she'd look *precioso*. Tell me I'm not lying."

I laughed. I couldn't help it.

I didn't eat lunch with Marwa. Mr. Gallagher was hovering around her, and I figured he'd make sure she settled in. As I walked by her table, she waved tentatively, but then Mr. Gallagher asked her a question. When she turned to answer him, I walked away quickly. And then I got very busy and I tried not to think about her for the rest of the afternoon.

Besides, Juliana occupied a big part of my mind. *She was leaving Glen Meadow!* I could hardly believe it. There are some people who don't like you and you don't like them back. It was pretty much that way with me and Juliana. I especially didn't like the way she sized me up every time she looked at me.

One day last year I'd asked Winnie about it. "What's Juliana looking at?"

"What do you mean?"

"She keeps staring at me in a weird way. Like there was something wrong with how I look."

"I don't know. Let's see." Winnie had checked me out from head to toe. "Well, it could be your outfit. Maybe you shouldn't wear those colors together."

"What's wrong with these colors? And why does she even care what I wear anyway?"

Winnie had shrugged. "I'm just telling you because you asked me. It's her problem, not yours. If you want to wear purple with orange, you go right ahead. This is a free country."

But that hadn't made me feel any better about Juliana.

Stinky Lunch

I didn't have long to rejoice. The very next morning, just as our bus pulled up to the school, I saw Juliana getting out of her father's sports car.

"Winnie, look!" I cried. "She's back!"

Winnie leaned across me to peer out the bus window. "Yup. You're right."

"But you said she was moving away! Were you making it up?"

"I wasn't. Honest. I guess she isn't moving after all," Winnie said. Once we were inside the school, we hurried toward our hall. Juliana was standing in front of her locker.

I took a deep breath and stepped closer. I simply had to know. Perhaps she was leaving at the *end* of the week?

"Oh, h..hi, Juliana." I tried to make my voice sound casual. "Winnie said she heard you were moving."

"Don't you wish!"

I emptied my backpack into my locker, just four doors down. "She heard you were switching to Sky Vale."

"To where?"

"Sky Vale," I repeated. "A private school?"

Juliana rolled her eyes. "I don't know where Winnie gets her information. I'm not going to Sky Vale or any other private school. I wish I were, though." Juliana banged the locker door shut and walked away.

"Why don't you go then, if you feel that way?" I muttered under my breath.

I marched into homeroom and jabbed Winnie on the shoulder. "How could you get it so wrong?" I cried. "You said Juliana was going to Sky Vale!"

"Oops! *Perdóneme.* I guess I made a mistake," Winnie replied. "Maybe she's going skiing in Vail."

"You got me all excited for nothing," I groaned. "You should have made sure first."

"So she's staying. What's the big deal?" Winnie started coloring the maps for our project.

"It's a big deal to me. She hates me. You know that!"

"I don't actually know that, Aliya," Winnie said. "You've got to stop being so sensitive."

I tried to sneak past Marwa's table at lunch, but she saw me. Her hand brushed my shirt sleeve. "Hello," she said.

Her lunch box was half open. Inside, I could see the Syrian bread packed with feta, lettuce, and olives. The cheese smelled really strong, like Heba's lunch at the Islamic Center.

I couldn't think of anything to say. "Um…how's it going?" I asked.

"It's going okay."

Some kids sitting nearby held their noses and pointed at Marwa's lunch. She didn't seem to notice.

"You dropped some." I pointed to a white glob by her feet.

"Sorry," she said, scooping it up with her napkin.

"They're serving chicken nuggets today," I said. "You should try them sometime."

"I can't. They're not *halal.*"

"Oh."

"You don't mind not eating halal?" She looked at my tray.

"It's okay with my family." I felt a little squirmy, like I'd been caught doing something illegal.

"We're pretty strict in our house," Marwa told me. "I could order on macaroni and cheese days, though. They have that here, right?"

"Yeah," I said.

"Or I could get PBJ or a salad or a baked potato. But this is my favorite lunch. Want to try some?" She scooted her chair over so I could sit next to her.

Winnie was saving me a seat, but I *had* promised Mrs. Holmes I'd be nice to Marwa. I sat down. "Doesn't the smell bother you?"

"It's just cheese," Marwa said, but she closed the lid of her lunch box.

A long stretch of silence followed. I moved the chicken around my plate with my fork, wishing I could join Winnie and the others. When Maggie and Sarah walked by, it was a perfect opportunity for a getaway. I called out to them, "Hey, you guys. Want to sit here with Marwa?"

"Sure," Maggie said, and I leapt up.

"You don't have to go," Marwa said. "There's plenty of room for all of us here."

"It's okay," I mumbled as I picked up my tray. "I'll see you later." I walked away quickly without feeling too bad. At least she had company.

"What were you two talking about?" Winnie asked when I sat down.

"Not much. We don't have anything in common."

"What's she eating?" Leah waved her hand in front of her nose. "It's stinking up the whole place."

"It's some Middle Eastern food," I said.

Madison peeled the plastic wrap off her sandwich.

"Ham again?" I said. "You have that almost every day."

"You should try it. It's really yummy!"

"Marwa won't eat chicken nuggets," I said.

"Why not?" Leah asked.

"It's not halal."

"What's halal?"

Now I sort of wished I'd kept my mouth shut. "It's got to do with food rules for Muslims," I explained. "You know— we're not allowed to eat pig, for one thing. That's why I don't bring ham sandwiches."

"We don't eat pork either," Leah offered. "And we keep kosher in our house."

"That's kind of like us," I said. "At least some of it."

"*Mmm-mmm.* Pig is *sooo* tasty!" Madison held up her sandwich. "We can eat just about anything."

"I won't eat sardines and asparagus and artichokes," Winnie said. "But I love potato chips and I'd be so mad if someone told me I wasn't allowed to eat them!"

Leah turned back to me. "You don't eat ham, but you eat chicken nuggets. But Marwa doesn't eat chicken nuggets. Does she eat pork?"

"I bet you anything she doesn't," Madison said.

"Well, who's right here?" Leah asked. "Marwa or Aliya?"

I jabbed my fork into my chicken. It was cold and limp and I wasn't hungry anymore.

Carly

At lunch the next day, Winnie, Madison, and Leah were in the middle of a deep conversation when I sat down to join them.

"'This year's party will blow your minds clear to the troposphere!'" Madison said. "Those were her exact words."

"Her parties are the best," Leah added. "I can't wait to go!"

"What are you talking about?" I asked.

"Are you going?" Madison slipped over to make room for me at the table.

"Going where?"

"To Carly's birthday party."

"She's having a party?" I was completely surprised.

"Aren't you going?" Leah asked.

"I didn't even know about it," I said.

"That's weird," Winnie said. "I don't see why she wouldn't invite you. She's known you since third grade."

No one said anything. But they were avoiding my eyes; they were probably feeling pretty bad for me. I bit down on my lip so hard, I could taste blood. Winnie was the first one to break the silence.

"I know what happened," she said, snapping her fingers. "Remember that day when you left early?"

I did remember. Mom had picked me up for a dentist's appointment.

"Well, Carly passed out the invitations later that afternoon. And you, *senorita*," Winnie went on, "you were *not* there and then she got sick. See?"

"But nobody told me about it? It doesn't make sense."

"I guess we thought you already knew," Leah said.

"Yeah, we sort of forgot about the dentist," Madison mumbled.

"I wouldn't worry," Winnie said, taking a sip of her milk. "You *are* invited. Trust me."

Winnie always made me feel better. Carly had just forgotten to give me my invitation. I calculated quickly in my head. The birthday party was on a Ramadan Saturday but that didn't matter. I'd skip the fast that day. Ramadan had thirty days of fasting; one less probably wouldn't matter too much.

In social studies, Mrs. Doyle assigned us our independent study project. The theme for this year was "Respecting Ourselves and Others."

"Uh-oh! More rainbows and mixed salads!" Winnie groaned.

"Huh?" I said.

"Don't you remember? The usual lecture how we all have our special qualities and differences...blah, blah, blah."

I nodded. We'd had assemblies about this kind of thing. We'd made flags from fifteen different countries last year, and they were still hanging in the cafeteria. And we'd even had an International Food Fair; everyone had had the chance to taste Amma's samosas and Winnie's *kimchee* and all sorts of other foods.

"We live in an increasingly multicultural society and it is important to be sensitive and respectful about our differences," Mrs. Doyle concluded.

Winnie gave me her I-told-you-so look.

I was walking back from the girls' room when I saw Marwa.

"Assalam alaikum!" she called.

"Oh, hi, Marwa," I muttered. "It's okay to say hello here at school."

"I waited for you at lunch today and yesterday and the day before." She fell into step beside me.

I shrugged. The smile on her face flattened a little.

"I can't talk right now," I said. I had already missed some of the math lesson.

"It'll only take a second. I was wondering if you'd like to come over to my house," Marwa said.

I did a double take.

"To…to your house?"

"Yes. To visit and maybe have dinner?"

"Who else is invited?" I asked.

"No one…yet," she said.

"What about Sarah and Maggie?"

"I'm asking you. My mom wants you to come. Will you?"

I scrambled for an escape route. "It depends," I said. "When exactly do you want me to come?"

"Anytime, really."

"I'm sort of busy for the next two weeks," I said.

"How about we have *iftar* together on the first Saturday of Ramadan?" she proposed.

I shook my head again. "I can't." That day was clearly out.

"You can't?"

"It's Carly's birthday," I explained. "She's having a party."

"Oh. That's okay," Marwa said. "I just thought I'd ask."

I hurried back to my room. While the teacher wrote our assignment on the board, I told Winnie about my conversation with Marwa. "I can't believe she asked me to come over. She's only been here one week. She doesn't even know me that well."

"That's because you haven't been spending a lot of time with her," Winnie said.

"And when am I supposed to do that? It's not like we're in the same classes."

"But still, it was nice of her to ask you. Maybe you should have accepted."

"Are you kidding?" I asked. "You seem to be forgetting Carly's party."

"Oh yeah, the party," Winnie said. "Right!"

I was already planning what I was going to wear and I had a pretty good idea about the gift I wanted to get. I'd probably have to do a little arm twisting at home; it would cost more money than Mom would want me to spend.

Steps to Success

I made sure I didn't spend too much time getting ready on Sunday morning. I didn't want to be late to the Islamic Center again. Lucky for me, the traffic was light and I got to Religion 2 a little early. The room was empty except for Sister Khan.

"On time today," she said, nodding in approval. "Ma'sha Allah!"

I sat in the last row and waited for my friends. I couldn't wait to talk to Nafees again. At night, I'd lie in bed and think about her kissing Marcus, the blue-eyed boy with a ponytail. After a while Marcus would change into Josh and Nafees into me. And then I'd get goose bumps all over.

"Scoot over," a voice said.

I jumped. It was Nafees. "Oh, hi," I said. "How's your new boyfriend?"

"Just dandy," she replied. "How's yours?"

"I don't have a boyfriend."

"Yeah, too bad," Nafees said. "But don't give up just yet. You might get lucky some day."

Amal plopped down beside me, grinning broadly. "Hey, you two!" she chirped.

"Hey yourself," I said. "What's up? How did it go?"

"What?"

"You know…that." I pointed to her hijab. "What did the kids say at your school?"

"Oh this? It was no big deal." Amal tucked a stray lock of hair back under her green scarf. "They asked a few questions and then everyone went about their business."

Nafees turned to me. "And exactly what did you think would happen?"

"Oh, I don't know," I said. "It's a big change for them, after all."

"For them?" Amal exclaimed, frowning. "I'm the one in hijab, remember?"

I let that sink in. "You're right. Weren't you the tiniest bit nervous?"

"Oh boy!" Nafees grunted, obviously impatient with my question.

Amal stared her down and looked back at me. "A bit," she confessed. "But by the end of the day my friend said she wasn't even paying attention anymore!"

"You mean she got used to it?" I asked.

"Uh-huh," Amal said.

Sister Khan rapped on her desk, and we all faced front.

I managed to keep my mind off blue-eyed boyfriends and hijabs by concentrating on the lesson for the day: the importance of the five daily prayers.

Ten minutes before the end of class, Sister Khan told us about the Steps to Success assignment.

Everybody groaned. We had enough going on at school without additional Sunday school work.

"This sounds just as confusing as the independent study project I have to do for Mrs. Doyle," I grumbled.

"I don't get it," Sehr said. "Grown-ups are always thinking they can change kids by giving them stupid projects like this."

It was getting noisy in the room and Sister Khan rapped on her desk again. "What's the big problem, people? Why such high drama?"

"This is too hard, Sister Khan!" Heba said. "Why couldn't we write about Prophet Yusuf and his brothers who threw him in a pit or—?"

"People! Enough!" Sister Khan held up her hand. I could tell she was getting impatient. "This is Ramadan, no? And in Ramadan, we must ponder on how to make ourselves better human beings, no?"

"Yes, but—"

"No buts! So, back to the assignment. First step: You will think...hmm...how to make myself *new*? How to *improve* my old self in the month of Ramadan? Second step: When you know, then you will act upon it. Third step: When you finish acting, then you will write a *full* report. Okay? Sufficient explanation?"

Amal, Heba, Sehr, and I exchanged uncomfortable glances and Nafees rolled her eyes. Sister Khan's English was pretty good, but sometimes it was hard to understand what she meant.

"Can you maybe give us an example?" Amal ventured.

"Eh? Oh, she wants example. Okay. In Ramadan, what we do? We communicate with Allah, no? We try to get closer to Him, no?"

Everyone nodded.

"*Accha!* Good, good!" Sister Khan said. "So—"

"I think I get it!" I blurted out. "It's like prayers. They're a form of communication with Allah, right?"

"Of course, but—," Sister Khan began.

"Do you want us to keep a record of how many times we pray?" I pressed.

"Yeah!" someone said. "We could make some graphs or something."

"Graphs?" Sister Khan frowned. "No. No. No graphing. Listen to me, people. I ask for something…something…umm…a little bit deep, no?"

"Deep?"

"Yes! Deep and *meaningful*," Sister Khan said triumphantly. "*Tcha!* It is not only about numbers and counting and graphs, no?"

So, keeping a quick checklist was out.

"Please give us a clue, Sister Khan," Amal begged.

"She needs another clue?" Mrs. Khan was beginning to sound annoyed. "All right, all right. Hmm. It is like this… like a trip to a place where it feels good when you are there. No?"

That was a clue?

"Huh?"

"Like going to the movies?" Nafees snickered.

"Like going to get your nails done?"

Sister Khan rapped for silence. "People, people. You must get serious for a change, please?"

Someone asked if we could ask our parents for help.

"Okay. Okay. You will need all the help you can get, it looks like," Sister Khan conceded. "But first, read these instructions." She handed out sheets of paper with directions printed on them.

"How long do we get to do this?" I asked.

"You start today, maybe tomorrow. In March, April you finish up. In between you improve all the time. Plenty time to improve!" Sister Khan replied smugly.

"I'm not doing this," Nafees growled under her breath.

I described Sister Khan's project to Badi Amma and asked her to help me figure it out.

"Hmm," she mused, pulling on her chin. "It makes me remember the nice man on TV."

"What nice man?"

"You know him." Badi Amma deepened her voice. *"Make the clothes nice and clean. Buy New and Improved Tide!"*

"What?"

Badi Amma laughed. "I learn a lot from TV," she said.

"Get serious, Badi Amma!" I cried. "What does TV have to do with this?"

My great-grandmother smiled. "It is simple. This teacher wants a new and improved you. Very smart lady, that one!"

"She's not that smart," I grumbled. "She's not even a real teacher. She's only a volunteer. Besides, what's wrong with me? I'm fine the way I am!"

"What you want me to tell you then?" Badi Amma asked.

"Oh, I don't know. Sister Khan said something about communicating with Allah. Maybe you can help me with that."

Badi Amma hawked and spit into the disgusting can she kept close to her bed. I understood she needed to clear her lungs, but I still thought it was gross.

"Then sit down and write Allah nice letters," Badi Amma said, swiping a napkin across her chin.

"That's crazy!" I said.

"You ask, I give advice, but you don't take my advice," Badi Amma said. "So next time don't ask."

The doorbell rang. Badi Amma peered through the curtain. "Little Veenee is here," she announced.

"Hi, Buddy Ma!" Winnie chirped as soon as I opened the door. "What's new?"

"My chest still barks like a dog when I cough," Badi Amma answered.

"I'm sorry! Make sure you don't get sick again, okay?"

"Come, I show you what I keep on my mirror." Badi Amma shuffled toward her room and motioned for us to follow.

"Look," she said, gesturing at the mirror over her dresser.

"Gee, you still have the get-well card I sent you," Winnie said. "Buddy Ma, you're the best! I'm going to make you another one, okay?"

"Little Veenee, you the best. You are *acchi bacchi*."

Winnie turned to me. "What did she call me?"

"She called you a good girl," I explained.

"Gee thanks, Buddy Ma! You're ah-chee bah-chee too!"

"Good, good. Make this one here smart with her numbers like you," Badi Amma said. "She is very smart in other ways but not in adding and subtracting."

"Thanks a lot!" I muttered.

"Do you know your twelve times tables, little Veenee?" Badi Amma asked.

"Sure I do," Winnie said.

Badi Amma proceded to give her a quiz. "Twelve fourteens are?"

"What?"

"Twelve fourteens are?" my great-grandmother repeated impatiently.

"Whoa! We didn't go up that high!"

"Sixteen fours are?" Badi Amma shot out again, as quick as lightning.

"They didn't make us do the sixteens either, Buddy Ma!

46

And anyway, we're in fifth grade. We don't do tables as much anymore."

"They let us use our calculators on the really big numbers," I added.

Badi Amma ignored me. "Chinese people are suppose be very smart with numbers. I see them vin many, many competitions."

"Badi Amma!" I moaned.

"I'm half Korean, Buddy Ma," explained Winnie. "Not Chinese."

"Chinese, Korean, same thing!" my great-grandmother said.

After gathering up some snacks, Winnie and I headed back to the living room and made ourselves comfortable on the sofa.

"You'll never believe the homework our Sunday school teacher gave us this week," I told Winnie. I tried to explain the Steps to Success assignment.

"I have absolutely no clue what you are talking about," she said, peeling a banana.

"Part of it has something to do with talking to God," I explained.

"With your Allah?"

"Allah...God, same thing."

"So why does the project have to be about talking to God? It sounds pretty weird, if you ask me."

"Come on, help me out here." I was hoping she'd have an idea I could use. "Sister Khan said Ramadan was coming and we needed to get reflective."

"What's that?"

"You know, get serious and thoughtful about our lives and everything."

"You mean review stuff, the way Mrs. Doyle always wants us to do for our weekend math homework?" Winnie asked.

"I guess."

"What exactly does she want you to reflect about?"

"I don't know," I said. "That's the problem."

"Sounds *muy dificil*," Winnie said.

"About as hard as the ISP we have to do."

"Oh yeah, that."

I had two projects looming over my head—Mrs. Doyle's ISP and Sister Khan's Steps to Success. I had no clue what I was going to do for either of them. "I'm completely swamped," I groaned.

"Completely swamped and completely stumped!"

"You're not kidding!" I said.

After Winnie left, I went upstairs to my room. I kicked off my shoes and lay down in my bed. Zayd was watching TV downstairs and Badi Amma was in her room. Amma had run out to pick a few things from the grocery store. Except for the faint sound of the TV, it was pretty quiet in the house.

I held my body still and closed my eyes for a while. Then I got up and went to my desk. I rummaged in the top drawer for a notebook and pencil, and started to write.

Sunday, October 20
5:00 p.m.

Dear Allah,
    My brain is not working today. Sister Khan says we have to do this project called Steps to Success and I haven't figured it out yet. Between regular school, after school, and Sunday school, there is just too much work!
                    Yours truly,
                        A

I went back to my bed and stared at the ceiling for a while. Then I got up and went back to the desk.

Sunday, October 20
A little later

Dear Allah,
    A lot has happened recently. A couple of weeks ago, we got yelled at in the middle of the street by a crazy lady. It was totally unexpected and it was pretty scary too.
    Nafees has a boyfriend! I can't stop thinking about him, especially since I don't have one. Josh doesn't even know I exist.

Amal is starting hijab. I don't understand why she needs to do it but she seems pretty sure of herself.

Sehr was kind of sarcastic when I said I might fast only on weekends. (She should mind her own business!) Do You think it's wrong not to fast every day?

I'm so disappointed Juliana is not moving away after all! Winnie thinks it's no big deal, but I do.

I'm afraid everyone is invited to Carly's party except me. I'm going to write her a get-well card after I finish this letter.

Oh yes…M came to town. I wish she had stayed in Detroit.

Yours truly,

A

PS That's a pretty long list. It would be great if You would step in and do something.

I snapped the notebook shut and went downstairs to watch TV with my brother.

Invitations

"Hey!" I called out when Carly boarded the bus on Monday. "You're back!" She waved at me and plopped into a seat up front. I didn't get another chance to talk to her until we were at our lockers.

"You've been gone forever," I said. "Are you feeling better now?"

"Yup."

"I'm so glad you're back. I sent you a get-well card."

"I got it." She sounded tired. "Thanks."

"I bet you can't wait to do something fun now that you're better, like maybe celebrate somehow?" I was hoping to jog her memory about the party invitation.

But Carly only said, "You're not kidding!" She coughed in the crook of her arm and headed into homeroom, leaving me to stare at her back.

"Why didn't she mention her party?" I asked Winnie.

"Just go ahead and ask," she told me, but I shook my head.

Winnie threw up her arms. "I can't believe you. All you have to do is *ask* her."

"You ask," I pleaded. "Please, please, please? Promise me?"

Winnie let out a dramatic sigh. "You are such a chicken! Okay, cross my heart!" She marched into homeroom and headed straight for Carly's desk.

"Is Aliya invited?" she asked her, just like that.

"Invited?" Carly sounded confused.

That was a bad sign. I held my breath. Maybe Carly's illness had made her forgetful?

"To your party, silly," Winnie prompted.

"Er…" Carly looked uncomfortable. "Um…"

"What?" Winnie pressed on. "Is she invited? Yes or no?"

Carly tugged at her hair, twisting her body nervously.

I pulled at Winnie's arm. "It's okay," I whispered. "Drop it."

But Winnie didn't drop it. "You mean Aliya's not invited?"

"Winnie!" I hissed, getting hot in the face. "I don't mind, really."

Carly's face was red too. "Um…it's just that…er…my mom said I could only pick six kids because the day spa is expensive and…um… It was hard to include everybody, you know?" she offered weakly. "I'm really, really sorry, Aliya."

"No worries," I said. "I couldn't come anyway. You know…Ramadan and all?"

"Oh yes, Ramadan." Carly sounded relieved. "So it's okay with you then?"

"Sure thing," I said. "Why wouldn't it be?"

I was in a terrible mood by the end of the day. As I walked out to the bus, Marwa ran up. I didn't really want to talk to her but it was too late. She was already beside me.

"Hi, Aliya," she said. "Have you decided?"

"About what?"

"About having iftar with me?"

"I didn't have a lot of time to think about it," I said.

"I guess you're going to Carly's party then."

I searched her face, but saw no trace of sarcasm. "I haven't had time to think about that either."

"You can still come if you want," Marwa said. "I asked Maggie and Sarah too. I thought it would be nice for them to see what an iftar is all about."

I couldn't believe she said that so easily. Maggie and Sarah were practically strangers and she was inviting them to her home for something as different as an iftar!

"Um…I guess so," I mumbled. "Here's my bus. I gotta go. See you later."

I found an empty seat at the front of the bus and sat by myself.

Monday, October 21
8:00 p.m.

Dear Allah,

I can't believe Carly invited Ellen and Tracy, but not me! I'm so mad! I've invited her to all my parties. I shouldn't have sent her that get-well card!

M invited me over again but I'm pretty sure I'm saying no. I know what an iftar is and I also know it's not half as much fun as a visit to a spa. She asked Maggie and Sarah. I've never invited Winnie to an iftar yet and I've known her forever. Do You think I should have? After all, she's my best friend, right?

Yours truly,

A

PS If I tell Mom about M's iftar invitation, she's going to be mad that I turned it down.

Partners

"This stinks!" Juliana hissed when I pulled my chair over next to hers. Mrs. Doyle made us do word problems in math once a week. She assigned us partners so we could discuss the problems. I'd already worked with Winnie, Madison, Nathan, and Stevie, dreading the day I had to work with Juliana. And now here I was facing her, with no way to get out of it.

This week's problem had several complicated layers—all related to cooking a Thanksgiving turkey, using weight and cooking time per pound *and* elapsed time.

"This is pretty hard," I mumbled. "I'm much better at social studies."

"Yeah…whatever!" Juliana pushed the math paper away and folded her arms across her chest.

"Mrs. Doyle said we have to do this together," I said.

"So what?" Juliana said. "I'm not working with you! What do you care about a turkey problem? You don't even celebrate Thanksgiving!"

"I do too!" I insisted.

"No, you don't. You celebrate some other holiday. Rama-something."

"Ramadan," I said. "That doesn't mean that I don't celebrate Thanksgiving."

"You and that new girl with the funny headgear don't even know what Thanksgiving is."

"I do too. Why are you lumping me with her? I am nothing like her," I said under my breath.

"What's that?" Juliana cupped her hand around her ear. "You're mumbling."

"I am not," I said more forcefully.

I wondered if Marwa was into American celebrations. She'd lived in Michigan before she moved here, but she might not even be a citizen yet. "We're inviting a lot of family for Thanksgiving this year," I said, trying to get off the subject of Marwa.

Juliana snorted. "I bet your turkey is drenched in all those smelly spices!"

"It is not!" I said. "Our turkey is delicious."

"There's this Indian restaurant on Main Street and when we drive by, the smell is so gross I have to hold my nose!" Juliana turned her head away and acted like I wasn't there.

I wished math could end, so I could escape.

The moment the bell rang I gathered up my papers quickly, hoping I could find someone to help me later—someone who knew I celebrated Thanksgiving, liked spicy food, and didn't look at me like a bug she wanted to stomp.

Wednesday, October 23
4:30 p.m.

Dear Allah,

Why are some people so horrible? If I were good in math, I bet I'd be a lot nicer when other people needed help! And what's more, Juliana thinks I don't celebrate Thanksgiving. What a jerk! And that thing she said about the Indian restaurant? We go there all the time and we've never held our noses!

I am so mad I could punch her nose!

Yours truly,

A

PS Just so You know: <u>I worked out the problem on my own, without anyone's help!</u> I'm not sure if the answer's correct, but at least I tried.

I underlined the PS and flipped back to my old letters. As I read them, I realized they calmed me down a little bit, like a band-aid on a paper cut. It was the same calm that had swept over me in the Islamic Center when my forehead touched the prayer mat and the woman's ugly scream began to fade away. My Badi Amma was onto something. I was communicating with Allah and it was helping a little.

But I didn't feel any different. Not really. I was the same old Aliya. I played with my pencil, thinking. After a while I took my notebook downstairs to show Mom the letters. She read them quickly.

"You turned down Marwa's iftar invitation?" was the first thing she said. "Why?"

"Mom, there are other letters too. Did you read all of them?"

"You're still having trouble with Juliana?" she asked. "Is it getting worse? Why didn't you tell me?"

I squirmed in my chair. "I'm just writing about my life at school," I explained. "It's called communicating and that's what I am supposed to do."

"Hmm."

"Well?"

"I don't know... I don't see how your letters fit the assignment." She flipped through the pages again.

"What do you mean?"

"These are just complaints. Where's the action?"

"The action is that I am *writing* them, Mom," I said.

"Yes, but what are you gaining by writing them? Isn't it just an idle exercise?"

"*Kya?*" Badi Amma cocked her ear.

"Mom thinks these are no good, Badi Amma!" I shouted.

"What's no good?"

"The letters you told me to write for the project."

"She's supposed to be getting something out of it," Mom explained. "I don't see what she's learning by writing down a bunch of words. It's like she's sitting in a hole, writing about sitting in a hole, without trying to climb out. I don't see evidence of effort."

"Huh?" I asked. "What hole?"

"It's just a figure of speech, Aliya," Mom said. "I don't think Sister Khan wanted a laundry list of complaints."

"Come on, Mom!" I cried. "I'm not complaining. I'm communicating and there's a lot going on, as you can see for yourself!"

"So you are saying that Sister Khan wants you to write a diary?"

"Yes… No! I guess I don't know what she wants. Why don't you just help me a little, huh?"

My grandmother, who had been listening quietly, dried her hands on a kitchen towel. "Let me see those letters, *Meri Jaan.*"

Meri Jaan. My life. That's what Amma called me. I was as dear to her as her own life. She'd surely approve of my letters. I handed them to her. "Read them," I urged. "Tell me they're fine."

"Yes, yes. Come, come," Badi Amma commanded. "Read those letters out to me."

Amma got her reading glasses out of her drawer in the little alcove just off the kitchen and put them on her nose. She read the letters, first to herself and then aloud to Badi Amma.

I drummed my fingers and jiggled my leg a little. Badi Amma had better not be as hard on me as Mom was. It was her idea in the first place.

My great-grandmother listened with finger on chin, nodding her head from time to time. "Read one more time," she said, and Amma read the letters over, slowly and loudly.

"Hmm," Badi Amma mused. "Putting thoughts down is first step. Action follows soon after."

"See?" I turned to Mom, although I didn't fully understand what Badi Amma had just said.

When Amma got to the part I had underlined, Badi Amma's head bobbed faster. "There! Not all talk, action too!" she exclaimed. She turned to Mom. "Read again. Look carefully!"

Mom re-read the letters. "So there is. I missed those the first time," she admitted with a sheepish smile.

"Where?" I said, snatching the letters from Mom's hand. "What are you talking about?"

"The Little Veenee part," Badi Amma said. "It will be very good she comes for iftar, see? She will learn more about you."

"That's action?" I asked.

"*Hanh, hanh.*" Badi Amma smiled. "Big, big action hiding in a little line!"

"There!" I told Mom triumphantly. "Satisfied now?"

We finished our dinner and afterwards Mom helped Amma put away the dishes.

After the kitchen chores were done, we came together in the family room. Mom sank down beside me on the sofa and we looked through a magazine together. After a while she tossed it aside and turned to me. I knew she wanted to hear about school.

"So...Marwa invited you to iftar?" she began.

I winced. Why did she have to make such a big deal about it?

Zayd lay on the rug watching his favorite cartoons, but I knew he had one ear tuned to our conversation. "And you said no," he piped up. "That was rude. Right, Mom?"

"Says who?" I growled at him. "Just butt out of my business."

"I'd like to meet her," Mom said. "How's she getting on at school? Is she making friends?"

"I guess. Kids talk about her food, though, and they make fun of her hijab. Actually, I don't blame them. It's pretty embarrassing."

"Embarrassing for whom?" Mom asked. "Her, or you?"

"Why doesn't she just bring something else?" I said. "Like tuna fish, for instance."

"Tuna is smelly," Zayd said.

"Shut up!" I cried. "This conversation has nothing to do with you!"

"You should invite her over," Mom said. "I'm sure she'd appreciate that."

"And invite little Veenee too," Badi Amma added. "Come, come. Time for lessons." My great-grandmother heaved herself out of her armchair and scuffed toward the door. She wore fancy hotel slippers that Baba had brought her from one of his business trips. They were one size too large, but she loved them because they were a gift from her favorite grandchild.

"Couldn't we please skip Urdu today?" I asked.

My great-grandmother turned and scowled at me. "Come quickly!" she commanded. "Juldi!"

Last year Badi Amma had insisted that Zayd and I study Urdu with her every day for an hour. We had protested loudly. It had taken a lot of haggling but we'd finally got her to agree to forty minutes three days a week. We tried to get her to cut it down further but she didn't budge an inch even when I reminded her about after-school math and all the homework I had to do.

"Do I have to, Mom?" Zayd asked. "Urdu's hard and it's too squiggly to write!"

"When Badi Amma calls, you say, 'Here I come, Badi Amma!'" Mom told him. "And you better run, mister!" She glared at me. "That goes for you too!"

"Here I come, Badi Amma!" Zayd shouted. I followed him into our great-grandmother's room for another lesson on the thirty-two letters in the Urdu alphabet and how to write from right to left without leaving any gaps.

Spilled Lunch

I t doesn't make any sense," Winnie said. "Why is it an independent study project if Mrs. Doyle allows us to work with partners?"

"Maybe because we can do our parts independently and bring them together?" Actually, I thought it was a pretty good idea. Working with Winnie would make it a whole lot easier.

Only three hands went up when Mrs. Doyle asked if we had started working on the project: Juliana's, Nicole's, and Morgan's. Winnie and I looked at each other and shook our heads. Neither of us had made any headway yet.

As we left the classroom, I overheard Juliana talking with Nicole and Morgan about their projects. I walked closer to them, hoping to get some ideas for mine and Winnie's.

Juliana whirled around. "Excuse me," she demanded. "Are you trying to steal our plans?"

"I'm not stealing anything," I said. "I'm just walking to lunch."

"Yeah, right! Why would you walk so close to us if you weren't trying to eavesdrop?" She rolled her eyes. I heard the girls giggle as they hurried on down the hall.

Winnie caught up with me. "What are they laughing about now?" she asked.

"Juliana thought I was trying to steal their fabulous ideas. As if our project won't be just as good as theirs."

"I don't know why you worry so much about what she says. I'm sure we'll come up with something even better. I know—let's do something about lefties and righties! Adam's a lefty and I'm a righty. I could collect a lot of data at home and we could do a comparison and submit surveys and graphs."

"I don't know if that's such a great idea," I said.

"Why not? The project is about differences. Left-handed people are different. I can tell you that from experience— my brother's a lefty and he's so different, he borders on being weird!"

"I don't know, Winnie," I said. "It'll end up being only about you and Adam because everyone in my family is right-handed. Anyway, you'd be doing all the work."

The closer we got to the cafeteria, the more crowded the halls got.

"I really hope we don't have to wait forever to get lunch," I said. "I'm famished."

As I turned the corner I slammed into Austin. The impact knocked his lunch bag to the floor and his apple rolled away.

"What the…?" He turned around. "Hey, weirdo, are you trying to kill me?"

"I'm sorry," I apologized. "It was an accident."

I could hear people laughing as he dropped to his knees, trying to rescue his apple. "I'll get you for this," he snarled. "Just you wait!"

"Come on," said Winnie, pulling me away. "He knows you didn't mean to run into him." We got into the lunch line and inched forward, putting food on our trays. Winnie headed to our table while I was still digging in my pockets for my lunch money. "Wait up!" I cried, but she was already gone. I glanced around the cafeteria.

Marwa was sitting by herself again.

"Eww…gross!" someone whispered.

"Nice headgear!" someone else said.

"Aliya?" Marwa called as I walked by her table. "Wait a sec."

"What's up?" I asked, slowing down a little.

"Well, I…"

I felt conspicuous there in the aisle; I didn't want Austin to spot me. "Um, Winnie's saving a seat for me."

"Okay," she said. "I just wanted to tell you that I talked to him just now."

I stopped. "Talked to whom?"

"I told Austin I saw the whole thing," she said. "I told him it was an accident and you didn't mean to knock his lunch down."

I was astonished. "When?"

Marwa shrugged. "While you were in line."

"You didn't have to do that!"

"I just thought…well…it *was* an accident."

"You should have kept out of it," I said. What if Austin was even madder now?

"I was trying to be helpful." She looked into her lunch box. "You seemed pretty upset."

"It's all right," I said. "I wasn't *that* upset."

Marwa shrugged again. "At our old school, they taught us that it's wrong for a bystander not to speak up. I was trying to stand by you."

"Thanks," I said, walking away. "But I could have handled it myself."

Monday, October 28
4:40 p.m.

Dear Allah,

What's with M? She won't leave me alone! I don't need her help. I've been here a lot longer than she has and I can handle things just fine, thank you very much! Who does she think she is, butting into my business?

Yours sincerely,

A

PS I bumped into Austin and his apple rolled away and everyone laughed when he chased it because it was so funny, except he didn't think so and now I think he is going to make my life really miserable.

PPS And Juliana thinks she's so smart! I can't wait to wave my project in her face. I will, just as soon as I know what it is!

When Mom came home, I told her about Austin's apple.

"What's wrong with that boy?" she said angrily. "I'll talk to Mrs. Holmes about it first thing tomorrow."

"Oh, Mom, please don't," I begged. "It won't do any good. Besides, if he finds out, it'll get worse. I'm just going to stay out of his way."

"You shouldn't have to do that," Mom said. "Mrs. Holmes will put a stop to his bullying."

"It's not that easy, Mom. Let's just forget the whole thing."

Hoping to distract her, I showed Mom my latest letter. She read it more carefully this time.

"I'm writing about what bothers me the most," I explained.

"I can see that, honey," she said.

"Well?"

"Well…you're still missing the point," she began.

"What do you mean?" I cried. "Aren't I doing a better job? Amma and Badi Amma think I am."

"At the risk of sounding harsh, your letter reads like a lament from a hole," she said.

"I don't understand. You keep talking about a hole. What hole? What lament?"

"Don't you see?" she asked. "There's still a fair amount of negativity here and very little that's upbeat and positive. It would be nice to see some change happening…some forward steps."

"I tried to vary my beginnings," I pointed out.

"I'm not talking about that kind of change," Mom sighed. "Your writing skills are fine. I just think your project is supposed to reflect some sort of personal growth."

"Change! Growth! New! Improved!" I yelled. "I don't get it! What do people want from me anyway?"

"To know that you are clear about the point of the assignment, for one thing," Mom said.

"Mom, it's not a science project with hypotheses and data analysis and conclusions and controls and variables and all that. I know the point. The point is to talk to Allah, and that's what I'm doing."

"There has to be more than just talk." Mom ruffled my hair. "That's all I am saying."

And even though she said it kindly, I couldn't help wondering. Were my letters really no good? Was I on a completely wrong track?

I took the notebook back to my room, tossed it in my desk drawer, and banged it shut.

Baba and Mom

Only three days remained until the start of Ramadan. I'd packed two sandwiches in my Sunday school bag; I guess I hoped my body could store up fuel to help me get through the times with no food.

Sehr unwrapped her sandwich and took a big bite. "Are you fasting on school days or are you going to chicken out again like last year?"

I wanted to tell her to mind her own business. Instead I repeated what Amma always told me. "'Allah gives full credit for our good intentions.' Don't you know that?"

"But you're a whole year older now. Don't you even want to give it a try?" Sehr turned to Nafees. "Don't you think I am right?"

"Oh, leave me alone," Nafees growled. Usually she was eager to give her opinion but today she didn't have much to say. She'd spent most of Religion 2, Arabic, and Quranic Reading doodling in her notebook.

Amal nudged Nafees with her elbow. "What's the matter with you?"

"Go ahead, Nafees," I said. "You can tell me what you think. I can take it."

Nafees turned on us. "Can't a person have a private moment without being bombarded with stupid questions?"

Amal, Sehr, and I looked at each other. Something was definitely wrong.

"Sorry," Amal said.

"What's going on?" Sehr looked concerned.

"I can't believe my stupid parents," Nafees muttered.

We waited for her to go on. By now we were used to her occasional rants, like a volcano erupting from time to time.

"They found out about Marc." Nafees slapped her lunch box closed. "And now they're being total jerks about it!"

Amal gasped. "How did they find out?"

"It was my idiot sister eavesdropping again. And thanks to her, I'm grounded for life! I hate her and I hate them! I hate them all and I hate my life!"

I felt sorry for Nafees. This time, she had a good reason for her dramatic outburst. If I was her and Marc was Josh and Mom and Baba had put their foot down about him, I'd be hopping mad too.

That evening, Baba returned from Detroit and we had dinner together like a proper family. Zayd and I never got used to our father being away so much. We always looked forward to his return—and not just because he brought us back nice things. Badi Amma loved the samples he brought her from the hotels—especially the eye masks. She also had an excellent collection of monogrammed slippers and little tubes of toothpaste, but she let Amma keep the sewing kits because she couldn't see well enough to mend our clothes anymore.

Baba filled his plate with spiced spinach and lamb curry. Amma had cooked his favorite foods to welcome him home. "I almost missed my return flight." He broke off a piece of flat bread and scooped up curried lentils as we waited patiently for the rest of his story. "They put my suitcase through the special X-ray machine. This was before I got to the security line, mind you."

"Why'd they do that, Baba?" Zayd asked.

I turned on my brother. "Don't you know anything?"

Mom passed Baba more *roti*. "Might it have anything to do with your Muslim name?"

"I waited for better than fifty minutes in that darn security line," he continued, ignoring Mom's question. "They puffed air at me and pulled me aside at the gate. They called it a random check."

"Yeah, right!" Mom snorted.

"It is getting pretty tiresome," Baba conceded.

"The surveillance…the Patriot Act," Mom said. "It makes me nervous, all of it."

"We are law-abiding," my father said. "You have nothing to worry about."

"That may be true, but in some ways, it's the kooks on the street I fear the most," Mom said with a sigh.

"Like the woman who screamed at us?" Zayd asked.

"What woman?" Baba asked.

I told him about what had happened on the way to the Islamic Center.

"I know it was upsetting. But it's best not to take it too personally." Baba was trying to smooth everything over like he always did.

"Hello?" Mom scowled at him. "Get your head out of the clouds and take a peek at the real world, please?"

But Baba only smiled.

"I bet some kid's going to cause trouble about Marwa's hijab," I said. "I don't understand why she has to wear it to school."

"It would be a big shame if her hijab caused trouble," Mom said.

"Don't worry," Baba said, looking straight at me. "Marwa's hijab will not get *you* in trouble."

Mom shook her head slowly. "I don't know anymore," she said. "It's sure unnerving to be singled out."

"Your friend seems like a gutsy little girl," Baba said to me.

"Marwa's not exactly a friend," I muttered.

"Oh?"

I changed the subject. "Guess what, everyone? I've made a decision. I'm going to fast during Ramadan this year."

"On school days?" Baba and Mom asked together.

I nodded.

"But, Meri Jaan, why not wait until the weekend?" Amma asked.

"If younger kids can do it, then so can I." Now that I'd decided to fast, I didn't want to be talked out of it.

Mom turned to Baba. "I should think she needs to stay sharp for math, right?"

"Yes, yes," Badi Amma interrupted. "She needs to get good at her numbers. Aliya, nine fourteens are?"

"Quit it, Badi Amma," I cried. "I'm not practicing math now." I looked over at my father. "I want to fast on Wednesday. May I?"

"Go ahead, kiddo," he said. "Give it a shot."

But the day before Ramadan, I came home from school with the sniffles.

"I don't like the sound of that cough either," Amma said, putting her hand on my forehead. "Maybe you should stay home tomorrow."

"*I* want to stay home," Zayd cried.

"I don't know, Amma." I sneezed a couple of times. "I'll let you know how I'm feeling."

"I'm making roti and egg curry for *suhur*," she told me. "That will keep you nice and full for your first day of fasting."

"Eat, eat," Badi Amma insisted. "Big day tomorrow."

"Ah-choo!" I sneezed.

Sniffles

Mom came into my room very, very early the first day of Ramadan. "Wake up," she said in a cheery voice. "It's your first suhur."

"What time is it?" My head felt heavy and the light hurt my eyes.

"It's almost 4:15. You can eat your suhur and catch a few more winks later if you like. Amma's waiting downstairs with a nice big early breakfast. Hurry up and do your ablutions."

"Mom, I don't feel good." I sneezed. "I don't think I can do it today. I'll fast tomorrow."

"You're the one who was clamoring to start right away. You made such a commotion about it the other day!"

"I'm just not used to waking up this early. I'll do it tomorrow."

"Aliya!"

"I mean it, Mom. I'll fast tomorrow, I promise. Please let me go back to sleep?"

The bus slowed for Carly's stop and I bit into the breakfast bar Amma had thrust into my hand as I left. After Mom granted her permission, I had pulled the warm covers over my head and closed my eyes. I'd slept right through my alarm.

I missed suhur, I overslept, and now I was munching on a breakfast bar. Ramadan wasn't off to a great start.

"Aren't you supposed to be fasting?" Winnie asked.

"I didn't make it. I'll do it tomorrow."

"Oh." She sounded disappointed.

"I've got a really bad cold, okay? And when a person's sick, they're excused from fasting." I sneezed into a tissue. "But I'm fasting just as soon as I shake this off."

Carly sat down across the aisle from us. "I've got the best news!" she chirped. "Wait till you hear what it is!"

I looked out the window and acted as though I didn't hear her.

"It turns out Ellen can't come to my party!" she went on.

Whoop-de-doo. I still wasn't ready to pretend that everything was okay.

"So you can come after all! That's what I'm trying to tell you."

I whirled around to face her. "First you didn't want me to come, but now suddenly you do?"

"Please, pretty please? Say, yes? You *are* my friend. I swear."

"I don't know…"

"I really, really, really want you to come. We're going to Le Tropez for manicures. Then we'll get pizza. It'll be a lot of fun."

"I'll check with Mom," I said. "It's Ramadan, but she *might* let me come." It wasn't exactly a great feeling to be an afterthought, but maybe it was better than not being invited at all.

We were talking near the picnic benches when Marwa approached. "Can I join you?" she asked.

No one spoke for a few seconds, and then Winnie said, "Sure."

"I'm Marwa," she said, stepping into our circle.

"We know," Carly said. "Everyone told us about you."

"And we've seen you around," Leah added.

"You're kind of hard to miss," I said.

Marwa looked at me and then away.

"Do you like it here so far?" Madison asked.

"It's okay," Marwa said. "It's pretty much the same as in Detroit."

"You weren't at lunch today." I traced a large figure eight in the dirt with my shoe, avoiding her eyes.

"You ate lunch?" She looked surprised.

"Sure." I knew why she was asking, but I didn't want to admit it. "Why wouldn't I?"

"It's just that it's Ramadan," she said softly.

"So why aren't you fasting?" Winnie asked me.

"I told you why," I said under my breath.

"No, you didn't," Winnie insisted. "You just said you weren't. You didn't say why."

"Hello?" I snapped. "The cold?"

"Anyway, I just came over to wish Aliya *Ramadan Mubrook*," Marwa said.

"What's that?" Madison asked.

"It means Happy Ramadan," I said. "That's what Muslims wish each other."

"Happy? When you're not eating all day?" Leah said. "That's weird."

"You say Happy Ramadan because it's a happy time," Marwa explained.

"I suppose you're fasting?" I asked, but I knew the answer already.

Marwa nodded. "*Al humdu lillah*," she said fervently. "Praise be to Allah. I've tried to do my best since I was ten."

As soon as I got home from school, I went straight for my notebook, like a moth to a light bulb. There were brand new feelings inside me clamoring to come out. I didn't care if writing them down was exactly right or wrong. And I didn't care that I might be crying in a hole either. Writing to Allah just made me feel better somehow.

Tuesday, November 12
5:00 p.m.

Dear Allah,

Carly said I could come to her party. I wanted to say no thanks, but they're going to a spa! I'll probably say yes later. But first I'll say something like, "My mom doesn't want me to, but I told her I had to because you were begging."

I have a question. Amma is at the library and Badi Amma's napping, so I can't ask them. Is it OK to fast and go to the spa at the same time?

M wished me Happy Ramadan. I was a little embarrassed because I wasn't fasting, but I had a cold! (I feel much better now.)

I think Mom is mad at me about not waking up for suhur. But my bed was warm and cozy and it was still pitch dark outside.

Back to M. Kids seem to have gotten used to her— at least a lot of them have, Maggie and Sarah included. But I overheard Juliana say something mean about her hijab to Nicole the other day. It almost felt like they were making fun of me too! I wanted to say something...and almost did.

Yours truly,
A

PS I am fasting tomorrow. Honest!

When the first fast ended at sundown, Amma had her iftar alone. Mom and Baba were still at work, Badi Amma was too old to fast, and I had chickened out. Amma bit into a plump California Medjool date and then she drank a glass of milk.

"That felt good!" She gave me a satisfied smile. "Eating a small amount at first helps prepare the stomach for a bigger meal after evening prayers."

I asked her about the visit to the spa on Saturday.

"Why would it be a problem?" she asked.

"I don't know... I just thought..."

"It sounds like a lot of fun. Do you think Carly would mind if I came too?" She winked at me and started clearing the iftar table.

"I'm sorry, Amma," I said.

Amma set the dishes back down. "Sorry for what, Meri Jaan?"

"For being a big chicken today."

"Is that what you were?" She sat next to me. "I thought you were sick with a nasty cold."

"Well, it was really hard to wake up at four in the morning," I admitted. "But I've been thinking about it all day and I am definitely fasting tomorrow."

"Looks like you've done some talking to yourself, hmm?"

"Sort of."

"And you've made some decisions? Some good ones?"

"I think so."

"*Shabaash!* Well done! You are moving in the right direction, Meri Jaan," Amma said. "And if these aren't baby steps to success, I don't know what is."

"So I'm off the hook with Allah?"

"You were never on the hook with anyone," my grandmother told me. "Especially not Allah."

First / Second Fast

The next morning, I was up and out of bed as soon as I felt Mom's hand on my shoulder. I ran to the bathroom to make my ablutions.

I washed my hands, the right one first, then the left, rinsed my mouth and nose, and splashed water on my face. Next, I washed my arms to the elbows, passed a wet hand over my hair, a wet finger in my ear, inside and out, and finished up with my feet, first the right one and then the left.

Amma was waiting with a big breakfast. She made me eat a whole roti with delicious egg curry so I'd be well fortified for the day ahead. After suhur, I laid my prayer rug down facing in the direction of the holy *Kaaba*. I raised both my hands to my ears and began. "Allahu Akbar…"

Before I left for school, Amma assured me that I should go ahead and break my fast if I felt light-headed.

"Are you sure I'm allowed?" I asked.

"Ramadan isn't a punishment," Amma reminded me. "Only a challenge to be met, Meri Jaan."

"I am going to meet the challenge." I tried to sound confident, but it was comforting to know that there was a way out.

My mind was on a silvery crescent moon as I walked to the bus stop. The air was chilly and my fingers were numb. My early breakfast was now a distant memory. Amma always said people feel the cold the most when they are the hungriest—and I was freezing!

"Darn!" I muttered. I fumbled in my pockets for my mittens, but I couldn't find them.

"You said darn," Zayd piped up. "You're not supposed to use swear words when you're fasting!"

"Darn is not a swear word, idiot!"

"You said idiot! You're not supposed to say that either!" Zayd dangled his lunch box in my face. "Amma packed me Doritos."

I pushed the lunch box away.

"Now you're getting mad," he sang. "You're not supposed to get mad when you're fasting."

I was ready to punch him, but just then Winnie came running with Adam in tow.

"Save me from this pest!" I moaned.

"You said pest!" growled Zayd.

Winnie set her backpack down beside mine. "Tch tch!" She wagged a finger at Zayd in mock anger before turning to me. "Why did I just do that?"

"He's being his usual obnoxious little self," I explained.

With Adam to keep him company, Zayd's attention got diverted and he left me alone. Thankfully I turned back to Winnie.

"I'm fasting," I announced, hoping it didn't sound too much like bragging.

"Cool! I'm impressed," she said, popping her gum. "Hey, can you chew gum while you're fasting?"

I shook my head.

"Weird!"

"It's not that weird," I said. "Amma says it's all a matter of self-discipline."

"I guess it's like staying away from cookies and chips when you're supposed to be dieting."

"Where's the stupid bus?" Zayd shouted. "I'm cold!"

"Yeah," Adam yelled.

"Quit it!" I snapped. "It'll be here when it gets here. Sheesh!"

"She said sheesh," Zayd told Adam. "She's not supposed to talk like that when she's fasting."

It was pointless to argue, so I turned away from him. The nip in the air made my nose cold and like my brother, I longed for the warmth of the bus. I searched the sky for the Ramadan moon no longer there.

"A moon with a happy mouth," I said, half to myself.

"Huh?" Winnie squinted skyward. "What? Where?"

"It was in the sky last night," I said. "It signaled the start of Ramadan, sort of with a smile."

"Weird," Winnie said and popped her gum. She blew on her hands and stamped her feet.

"Brr! Where *is* the bus? It's sure taking its—"

"Hey, everybody! I can see it. It's coming!" shouted Zayd.

By snack time I was starving. Winnie ripped open a bag of chips and a tangy smell rushed out. Immediately, my mouth watered. Fasting was going to be a lot harder at school, surrounded by everyone's food.

"These are great! Want one?" she offered.

"No thanks. I'm fasting, remember?"

"Oops, sorry! I forgot!"

"It's okay…no big deal." I couldn't look away. I watched as she finished the whole bag and licked red crumbs from her fingertips.

Mrs. Doyle said I could go back to the classroom and use the computer during lunch. I tried to keep my mind on a game about the water cycle, but I kept letting the little water droplets get eaten up by ravenous creatures. Gobble, gobble. The game wasn't helping at all. Hot and crisp French fries, pizza, and fudge brownies popped into my mind with every gobble.

In spite of the chilly weather, I decided to go outside for the rest of the lunch period. When I passed the empty cafeteria, the lingering smells of lunch drifted out the door. I inhaled deeply, and pressed down on my stomach to kill the growling.

The cold air made me catch my breath. I saw Marwa at the picnic bench with Maggie and Sarah. Her hijab was fastened neatly and securely and I supposed her ears were a lot warmer than mine right now.

They saw me and waved. I went over.

"Winnie said you're fasting today," Marwa said.

I nodded. "I stayed in the classroom during lunch."

"Me too. I did some work for Mr. Gallagher."

"How are you holding up so far?" I asked.

"Fine," she answered. "Al humdu lillah. And you?"

"Great, just great. It's a breeze."

"I don't know how you two can do it," Maggie said. "I could never go without food and water for a whole day."

"Me neither," added Sarah.

"Marwa invited us to her house for"—Maggie turned to Marwa—"what's it called again?"

Marwa smiled. "Iftar. It's the breaking of the fast."

"Are you going then?" I asked.

Maggie shook her head. "I can't."

"I'm not 100 percent sure yet," Sarah said.

I pulled my hood up. "I'm freezing. I better keep walking to warm up." I told them goodbye and headed toward the other side of the playground, where Winnie, Madison, Leah, and Carly stood.

"It's about time," Winnie announced. "Where've you been? You've been gone for ages."

"I was at the computer while you were eating, and then

I stopped to talk to Marwa."

"You're getting pretty cozy with her, aren't you?" Carly asked.

"I was just being nice."

"You didn't give me an answer," Carly said.

"I did too," I said. "I told you I was just talking with her."

"I mean about my party. You didn't tell me if you are coming or not. If you're not, then I need to ask someone else."

My mind had been so preoccupied with food that I'd completely forgotten about the party. Mom had said I could go, even though she'd made it clear that she thought a spa was too frivolous for someone my age. Badi Amma said it sounded like fun once I explained to her what a manicure was.

"Yeah," I said. "I'm coming."

Later that afternoon, I passed Marwa in the hall. I was so hungry, I thought I was going to faint.

"Math's next," she said cheerily.

"Whoop-dee-doo," I said under my breath. Hadn't she figured out by now how much I hated math?

"You're pretty grouchy today," she observed.

She was right, of course, but when she said it, I felt even grouchier. "I guess not everybody can be like you."

I dragged my feet into the classroom and slumped into my seat. I glared at my math book, wishing it was a big sandwich...or even a stale breakfast bar. Ramadan was supposed to teach a person about patience and compassion and remind them about people who have a lot less food to eat, but so far it was only reminding me about how hungry I was.

My stomach growled so loudly on the bus that I couldn't think straight. Winnie chattered on and on, but her words were a big blur until she asked if I was hungry. I nodded my head. I was ravenous.

"Me too," she said. "Here." She thrust a yellow bag in my face. I breathed in the oniony smell.

"Thanks," I said, and popped a crisp golden ring in my mouth. A Funyun had never tasted so good.

"More?" Winnie held out the bag again.

"Sure." I was just about to toss another one into my mouth when Winnie screeched. "Wait! Aren't you supposed to be fasting?"

I froze. The golden ring was an inch away from my tongue. My heart jumped into my mouth and I dropped the Funyun like a hot potato. I had forgotten! I had really and truly forgotten!

Zayd spun around in his seat. "You *ate*?"

The rumbling in my stomach was shocked into silence.

"Uh-oh! You made a big boo-boo, right?" Winnie said.

"What are you going to do?"

I had no idea. I'd been so good all day. I'd gotten up right on time that morning. I'd avoided the cafeteria during lunch, turned away from Pringles and Hershey Bars and Doritos during recess, and walked past the water fountain in the afternoon. Now, just an hour or so shy of sunset, I had gone and ruined everything.

"I don't know!" I groaned. "I'll ask my grandmother."

Zayd told on me the second we stepped inside, but my grandmother pooh-poohed the whole matter. "Allah gives full credit for one's intentions and yours were flawless, Meri Jaan."

"I ate a curry puff in the middle of my fast when I was this high." Badi Amma held her hand three feet off the ground.

"What's a curry puff?" I asked.

"You never have curry puff? *Arre arre*! Curry puff is special vegetable patty, very nice. Mint chutney inside…so tasty." Badi Amma smacked her lips.

"Hey, Amma," Zayd said. "Let's eat curry puffs for dinner tonight."

My dear grandmothers had coaxed a smile out of me, but my brother hadn't finished his tattling.

"Aliya ate Funyuns on the bus!" he announced as soon as Mom returned from work, like I'd wolfed down a whole bag on purpose. And then he added, "I'm telling Choti Dahdi when she comes and she's going to be sooo mad!"

The crimson streaks faded from the sky and dusk settled over everything like a smooth, dark blanket. My grandmother consulted the timetable stuck to the refrigerator and told us that sunset was five minutes away. I ran upstairs to make the required ablutions for the prayer that would soon follow.

"Make sure you wash in and around your ears," Amma reminded me.

"I know!" I cried. I was so hungry that I didn't think I could last another minute.

I splashed water on my face three times and rinsed my mouth. I washed my arms to my elbows and last of all, I washed both my feet in the bathtub.

"It's time!" Amma called.

"Coming, Amma!" Nothing and nobody could keep me away from my iftar now! I ran downstairs two steps at a time and made a beeline for the table, but Zayd had already beaten me there.

"Here she is," Badi Amma announced grandly, "the brave, fasting girl!" She motioned me to sit.

"You better not eat until I do," I warned my brother, who was eyeing the many delicacies Amma had prepared especially for me.

"Not to worry," Amma reassured me. "There's plenty for everyone."

And she was right! My grandmother had enough food to feed a herd of hungry elephants.

"*Dua, dua,*" Badi Amma reminded me. Dutifully, I cupped my hand in front of me and quickly recited the short fast-breaking prayer at the table with Amma.

Then I lunged for the food. I bit into a soft, sweet date and ate lentil dumplings swimming in yogurt sauce. The minced-meat samosa was flaky and the fruit *chaat* was out of this world!

"Don't gobble," Badi Amma instructed. "You must chew your food like this."

"Badi Amma, you look like a fish," Zayd giggled.

"Kya bole?" my great-grandmother asked.

"Nothing," Amma said, giving Zayd a warning stare.

After iftar, we got ready for the evening prayer. With mats angled properly and with bodies facing the holy Kaaba, we touched our thumbs to our earlobes and began with an Allahu Akbar. I tugged on my slippery scarf to keep it perched on my head, but it just wouldn't obey. I finally let it go and turned my full attention to Allah.

Praise be to Him, my first fast had come to an end, glitches and all!

We sat down to dinner as soon as Baba returned from work.

"How was your first fast?" he asked.

"Pretty good," I answered.

"She ate a Funyun on the bus," Zayd piped up.

"Stop being such a tattletale, you jerk!" I shouted.

"She called me a jerk, Baba!" Zayd said. "Is she allowed to do that when she's fasting?"

"I'm not fasting now, double jerk!"

"Quit it, both of you!" Mom ordered.

"A certain amount of amity would be welcome about now, eh?" Baba speared a chunk of chicken with his fork. "After all, it is a big day for us with Aliya fasting and it would be nice indeed to end it on a friendly note."

We ate in relative silence after that. It had been a long, hard day of fasting; I was tired and welcomed a little peace and quiet. I ate all the food on my plate that night.

Wednesday, November 13
8:00 p.m.

Dear Allah,

I did it!

For a while there, I wasn't sure, but I kept walking past the water fountain at school.

So, not counting the small accident on the bus, I'd say that I definitely did it!

Yours truly,
A

Weird Headgear

I was on a roll. Waking up early the next day was a lot easier and it was fun to eat suhur with Mom and Amma. We spoke in hushed voices so Baba's sleep wouldn't be disturbed. My father wasn't very regular about fasting—not because he was a bad person or anything, but because he was always making important decisions at his work and needed 200 percent energy. Badi Amma understood completely but it gave our Choti Dahdi one more reason to disapprove.

Amma had prepared another elaborate breakfast for me.

"I can't eat this," I mumbled. My dinner from the night before was still heavy in my stomach.

"Eat up, Aliya!" my grandmother urged. "And drink plenty of water to keep hydrated!"

"I've written a note to excuse you from P.E. today," Mom said. "Be sure to give it to your teacher."

That afternoon Winnie and I headed toward our lockers, glad to be going home soon. I wasn't looking where I was going and bumped into Austin again in the hallway.

"Hey!" he yelled. "I'm getting tired of you running me down!"

"I'm sorry," I muttered.

"Somebody ought to give you a speeding ticket."

"*Hooold* on!" Winnie intervened. "This isn't a road and I don't see cars or cops anywhere! Besides, she apologized."

"Apology not accepted!" Austin barked.

"I didn't see you," I said.

"So? Get a pair of glasses like that new girl with the weird headgear," he spat, "or your geeky friend here!"

"Are talking about me?" Winnie screeched.

Marwa closed her locker door and walked toward us. Her beige hijab looked great with her coral sweater. She held her head high, which made her seem taller than Austin.

"I don't see any other weirdo around." Austin made a big show of looking around until his eyes stopped at me. "Oh, my mistake. I see another one!"

"Cut it out!" Winnie said.

"What is it about my scarf that you find so strange?" Marwa asked. Her voice didn't shake like mine had.

"Everything!" Austin said.

"Oh. And what about that hat on your head?"

"Huh?" Austin took off his baseball cap and turned it around in his hand. "It's a New York Giants cap."

"It's something to cover your head with, just like my scarf. What makes mine weird and yours so great?"

Austin snorted. "Do you see anyone else wearing a scarf around here?"

"Just because you don't see a lot of people wearing something doesn't make it weird. Anyway, my hijab is not hurting you."

"You bet it is," Austin said. "It's hurting my eyes."

"That's too bad," Marwa said. "I can't help you there."

"I don't need help from you, so just butt out." Austin banged his locker door shut and stomped off down the hall.

Marwa slowly turned and walked away.

"Why don't you stand up for yourself like Marwa does?" Winnie asked.

"I don't know," I said, barely holding back the tears. I was furious at Austin. On top of that I was starving. "He's such a...such a..."

"I know you have to watch what you say when you're fasting," Winnie said. "But I'm not fasting, so I can say it for you. Austin is a complete loser and a total jerk!"

Friday, November 15
7:00 p.m.

Dear Allah,

Winnie's pretty impressed with M. "Why don't you stand up for yourself like Marwa does?" she asked me. I want to, but every time I try, I get a brain freeze and my stomach knots up inside and the words don't come out right.

Can You please do something to fix that? I am waaaiting!

Yours truly,

A

PS M's baseball-cap line was so clever. I wouldn't have thought of it in a million years.

Pepperoni Pizza

E arth to Aliya!" Carly snapped her fingers in my face. "You're a million miles away."

"I'm here," I said.

We'd already ordered our pizzas, but fifteen minutes remained before my fast would end. I kept my eyes glued to the clock and tried to will the time to move faster. I held up my hands to admire how pretty and glossy my fingernails were. The manicurist had painted stars on every other one.

The pizzas arrived, hot and steamy, and my mouth watered. "Go ahead," I told the others. "You don't have to wait for me."

No one waited. I couldn't blame them. Nobody likes cold pizza.

"A few minutes won't make any difference," Winnie said between mouthfuls. "Just go ahead and eat."

"I can't." I tried not to stare at the slices disappearing quickly from the pans.

"Hey, we should save some for Aliya," Winnie reminded the others.

"We are, we are," someone mumbled, but the mushroom slices were going pretty fast.

"Thanks, Winnie," I said gratefully.

"*De nada*. But it's best when it's hot."

"I know," I sighed. Time ticked by slowly. I kicked myself for not putting a couple of slices on my plate; now the pans were almost empty.

"We're saving you some," Madison said. "Don't worry."

I eyed the glass of soda waiting by my empty plate. My throat was dry; I could almost feel the cold carbonation. I drummed my fingers on the table. At last, the minute hand clicked to the precise spot on the clock.

"Okay, you guys," I announced. "I can eat now."

Carly slid the remaining pans to me. There were two pieces of mushroom and two pieces of pepperoni left. I grabbed a slice of mushroom. It had cooled down some but it still tasted pretty good to someone who hadn't eaten since dawn. I ate it quickly, and reached for the other one. After I finished, I was still hungry, so I picked up my third slice.

"That's pepperoni!" Winnie warned.

"I know," I said. "It'll be okay if I pick off the pepperoni."

"Did you have a good time at the party?" Mom asked.

"It was great," I said. Actually, it hadn't been all fun. It wasn't easy being extra patient and extra disciplined when everyone else could dive right in.

"What did you eat?" Zayd asked.

"Super-yummy-delicious pizza!"

Zayd pushed away his plate of rice and hamburger meat curry. "I want pizza," he whined.

I didn't blame Zayd for rejecting his supper. Mom made this dish at least twice a week. She'd varied it a little this time by adding green peas. But I wasn't through tormenting the little tattletale.

"Yummy yum yum!" I said.

"What kind was it?" Zayd asked.

"Mushroom and pepperoni," I said. "Yum!"

Mom looked up. "You ate pepperoni?"

"I took the pepperoni off. There weren't any more mushroom slices, and I was really hungry."

"Have I eaten pepperoni, Mom?"

"Pepperoni is made of pork, Zayd," she said.

"But Aliya ate it."

"Are you deaf? I said I peeled the pepperoni off!"

"Is she allowed to do that, Badi Amma?" Zayd asked.

"Kya bole?" My great-grandmother cupped her ear. "Allowed to do what?"

"IS SHE ALLOWED TO EAT PEPPERONI?" Zayd yelled.

Badi Amma turned to Amma. "What is this pepperoni?"

"I didn't eat it, idiot!" I yelled. I looked from Badi Amma to Mom to Amma. I had screwed up my first fast; I didn't want this one spoiled too. "Was my fast ruined, Amma?" I asked.

"Of course not, Meri Jaan," my grandmother replied. "Allah saw you remove the pepperoni."

Saturday, November 16
9:00 p.m.

Dear Allah,

    I messed up a little and I'm sorry. Everybody makes mistakes but they learn from them. I do feel better that You give credit for a person's good intentions. I don't mind telling You mine were all good.

Yours truly,

A

PS I sure am glad Choti Dahdi isn't around. She'd never forgive me, I bet.

Ideas

Winnie and I decided to take the long route to the office to deliver some papers for Mrs. Doyle. When we walked past the bathrooms, we saw that the doors were propped open and there were orange cones at both entrances. Mr. Belotti was in the boys' room, mopping the floor.

"Hey, Mr. Belotti, what's up?" Winnie called.

"What's up? I'll tell you what's up! Some punk stuffed wads of paper down the toilet. That's what's up!"

"Uh-oh!" Winnie said. "Is it bad?"

"It's Niagara Falls! That bad enough for you?" The rest of Mr. Belotti's words were lost under the slosh of his mop and the clank of his bucket.

"Mr. Belotti, what's that?" Winnie asked, pointing to the girls' room.

I poked my head in. Someone had scrawled words on the first stall:

JC loves J
J and JC together.

And not far below it, in the same handwriting:

M is totally weird
Ban crazy scarves and stinky cheese!
M, go home!

"*You* tell *me*, kiddo!" Mr. Belotti growled. "It's defacing school property, that's what it is!"

"That wasn't there yesterday," I said.

"No kidding!" Mr. Belotti said. "It's here now, and guess who's going to have to clean it all up?"

"It's too bad that you have to do it, Mr. Belotti," Winnie said.

"Yeah, Mr. Belotti," I added. "Some kids have no respect."

As we walked on toward the office, Winnie looked over at me. "That was about Marwa back there."

I nodded. My eyes had focused on the words right below the scribble about Juliana and Josh. Anyone would know that the *M* on the stall wasn't for Morgan or Marybeth or Madison.

"I'm sure glad Mr. Belotti will get rid of it before she sees it," Winnie said.

"But what if she's seen it already?" I asked. "She could have passed the open door just like we did."

"Yeah, that would be so terrible!" Winnie nodded. "Some kids can be so mean."

We delivered the papers to the office and waited for an

envelope to take back to Mrs. Doyle. As we neared our classroom we heard a familiar chime, followed closely by an announcement over the school intercom.

Attention, Glen Meadow students. The boys' and girls' restrooms in the upper wing are closed until further notice. If you need to use the restroom, please check with your teacher. Thank you for your cooperation.

We heard groans from the classrooms.

"Uh-oh!" I turned to Winnie. "Mrs. Holmes knows! Now we're in for it!"

A year ago, one of the school bathrooms had flooded. No one ever found out who did it or why, but it was a mess. It was closed for two days for repairs, and that meant the students on that hall had to go to the bathroom in the nurse's office. But that was only one toilet. This year, it was worse and Mrs. Holmes was livid.

The thing is, when something like this happens, you can never be sure who's responsible—but I had a pretty good idea.

"Hi," I said.

Marwa looked up from her book with a surprised look on her face. "Oh, hi!"

"Are you fasting?" I asked.

"Al humdu lillah," she answered. "And you?"

I nodded. "Are you planning to fast the rest of the month?"

"As much as I'm able to. And you?"

"I don't know, same for me, I guess," I said.

Marwa flipped the pages of her book with her thumb.

"Did Sarah come to your house for iftar on Saturday?"

Marwa shook her head. "Something came up and she couldn't make it."

I took a deep breath. "I'm sorry I didn't come either. It was really nice of you to ask."

"That's okay," Marwa said. "No big deal."

I inhaled again. "That was pretty brave of you…the other day…," I stammered. "With Austin, I mean."

"Oh that! Well—"

"You really told him off."

Marwa took off her glasses and polished them on her sleeve. "He *was* being an idiot," she said.

"Weren't you the tiniest bit afraid?" I asked.

"He had no right to talk about my hijab that way," she said.

It was the first time that word had been mentioned between us. And now that she had brought it up, I cleared my throat. "I was wondering…um…are you being teased about it? By anyone besides Austin?"

Marwa shrugged.

I waited for her to admit that kids were being mean. If she had, I might have told her about being called a weirdo by Austin or about Juliana rolling her eyes at me. But she didn't say anything. Maybe she hadn't seen the writing in the bathroom.

I looked straight into Marwa's face, instead of avoiding her gaze like I usually did. She seemed different without her glasses.

"What's the matter?" she asked, wiping at her cheeks. "Is there a smudge on my face?"

I shook my head. "Sorry," I said. "I didn't mean to stare. You have pretty eyes."

Monday November 18
9:00 p.m.

Dear Allah,

Something really strange happened today. When I was talking to M during recess, she asked me why I was staring at her. The first thing that occurred to her was that she might have a smudge on her face. Having a little dirt on her cheek worried her more than the scarf on her head.

Then I went deeper and I realized something else.

Her hijab doesn't scare her one bit.

But it scares me.

And it confuses me.

But she is completely OK with it.

Yours truly,

A

PS I thought I had something more to say but now I don't know what.

The next day, Marwa and I ran into each other on our way out to recess.

"Have you been helping Mr. Gallagher again?" I asked.

Marwa nodded. "He gave me a stack of math papers to look over."

"He's making you correct other kids' papers?" I asked. "Isn't that his job?"

"I don't mind," she said. "But I wish he'd give me something more interesting to do."

"Like what?"

"Oh, some sort of project, something I could do some research on."

I told her then about Mrs. Doyle's independent study project and explained how it was supposed to celebrate differences by showing respect for things like cultures, traditions, and abilities.

"That's exactly what I mean!" she said. "I hope Mr. Gallagher will assign a project like that. I'd love to do something where I could hop on the internet and *zoom*...take off!"

"Not me. I get stuck before I can take off," I said. "And right now, my head is empty. I can't seem to get going with my Sunday school project either. It's pretty complicated." I told her briefly about Sister Khan's Steps to Success but I didn't breathe a word about my letters.

We walked out into the nippy air.

Marwa blew on her hands. Her breath made cloud puffs in the air. "You could do something on Islam," she suggested.

"On Islam?"

"That's right."

"Er...I don't think that's such a good idea," I said.

"Why not?"

It wasn't a rude question. It didn't sound like a challenge either. But she just seemed surprised. But how could she even ask? Didn't she already know from the newspapers and the TV and everywhere else? Didn't she know people around here were angry at us? They didn't want to learn about our religion.

"Muslims aren't very popular these days," I said.

"You mean because of 9/11?"

"Yeah."

"Well, that's why you need to do it. Don't you see?"

"You're kidding, right?" I asked. "I don't want to call attention to myself."

"My dad says it helps when people talk things out. He's always going to interfaith meetings where they do that."

"I don't know..."

But Marwa went on. "My dad says it makes things clearer in people's minds when they have the right information and that can only happen when there is a conversation."

Like the conversation we were having right now? But

my mind was still cluttered with questions. What if kids hated it? What if they asked hard questions? What if I didn't know the answers?

"Just think about it," Marwa said

"I don't know. Maybe I'll talk to Winnie," I said. "She's my partner. She has a big say in this too."

"It's about time," Winnie called. "I thought you'd passed out from hunger and were in the nurse's office lying down."

"I was hurrying, honest," I said, dropping into the empty swing next to hers. The metal was icy under my hands and the cold breeze ruffled the collar of my jacket and made the tip of my nose numb.

"You were talking forever to Marwa," Winnie said, pronouncing it Mar-way. "I thought you'd never get here."

"It's Mar-wuh," I corrected her. "With an *uh* sound. And you've got to work on Badi Amma's name too."

"There's nothing wrong with the way I say Buddy Ma's name," Winnie protested. She practiced Marwa's name as she pumped the swing. "*Mar-wuh, Mar-wuh, Mar-wuh.*"

"Was my name hard to remember at first?" I asked.

Winnie looked at me like I was crazy.

"Well?"

"What's gotten into you?" she asked.

"Tell me, Winnie."

"I don't remember. I never thought about it. Okay?"

"Okay." I smiled. I was happy with her answer.

We swung back and forth in perfect timing, the creaks of our chains perfectly synchronized. Our jackets billowed out on every forward swing.

"You'll never guess what Marwa just told me," I said, pumping with my legs. The cold air lashed my face and made me catch my breath.

"No, but I bet you fifty dollars you're going to tell me."

"You know the project we're working on for Mrs. Doyle? Marwa thinks I should do something about Islam. Can you believe that?"

Winnie let her swinging slow down a beat. She seemed to be turning this idea over in her mind. "You know, that might not be such a bad idea," she said, excited now. "You could do that because that's the Muslim part of you and you could also do something on India because that's the Indian part of you and I'll do something about the Korean and the Jewish parts of me and Buddy Ma will help you with your part and I'll write to my Halmunee to help me with mine."

"Are you serious?"

"I'm completely serious," she said. "As a matter of fact, I love the idea! And you can tell that brilliant Mar-wuh girl that I said so!"

"What about the lefty project?"

"This one's a lot better," Winnie said. "Trust me."

I told Amma about Marwa's idea when I got home from school. She thought it was a wonderful plan.

"You could do a whole display," she said.

"Of what?"

"Of all the things that make you who you are," she replied.

"And what's that?"

"A tasty concoction of American and Muslim and Indian and sugar and spice and everything that is very nice."

Tuesday, November 19
7:30 p.m.

Dear Allah,

Winnie's really into M's idea! She's already written to her Halmunee in Seoul. She says Adam's pretty mad he doesn't get to be interviewed. I told her he'd get over it. I'm putting ideas together for my part. I've asked Baba to film me praying at the Islamic Center. I think the kids may be interested in how we do our prostrations together, shoulder to shoulder and in straight rows.

Yours truly,

A.

PS I hope there won't be too many tough questions. I'm keeping my fingers crossed.

PPS I hope M's dad is right about conversations opening doors.

Important Decision

Nafees seemed even grumpier Sunday morning. I figured we should stay a mile away from the subject of Marcus, so I asked about everyone's Ramadan and told them about mine, without mentioning the Funyuns and the pepperoni.

"You fasted on a school day?" Sehr asked. "Whatever made you change your mind?"

I thought I detected a little sarcasm. "I didn't change my mind," I said. "I made up my mind, actually."

"Same difference," Sehr said.

"No way. There's a huge difference."

Amal turned to me. "It's all about mind over matter, right?"

"Exactly!" I said. "And a positive attitude."

"Yeah!" Amal agreed. "It's all in the head. A lot of people don't realize that."

We traded Ramadan stories for a while, but Sehr didn't join in.

"What's wrong, Sehr?" Amal asked. And then Sehr told us a story about her sister that made us forget all about suhurs and iftars. The news was so horrible we didn't know what to say.

"Someone *pulled* the hijab off her head?" Amal sputtered. "Are you kidding me?"

"In broad daylight in the middle of campus. And trampled it on the ground," Sehr elaborated. "She's so upset, she can hardly sleep."

My stomach twisted up into a knot. "That's terrible!"

"She says she's giving it up. She's too scared to wear it in public now."

"It's not right!" Amal said. "It's simply not right!"

"What's not right?" Heba asked. "That she's scared? Or that she's given up the hijab?"

Amal shook her head. "It's not right that the whole thing happened in the first place. She wasn't hurting anyone, was she?"

I thought about Marwa. Was she scared when kids pointed at her and made fun? Had she seen the graffiti? I turned to Amal. "You should be careful. It could happen to you too."

"I don't think so," Amal said. "People at my school are very respectful."

"She gave up too quickly," Sehr muttered.

"What did you say?" I turned, not believing what I just heard.

"My sister gave up too quickly," she repeated more forcefully. "She should have stuck to her belief."

"She's giving up wearing the hijab, but she's not giving up being a Muslim, is she?" Amal asked.

"Nobody's saying that," Sehr snarled. "Still…"

It took me a minute to process everything. "But what if not everyone is that brave?"

"I don't care. I would have stuck to my guns," she replied.

I tried to imagine myself in her sister's shoes. Or Marwa's. "It's easy to say now," I told her. "You can never tell until it happens to you."

Nafees had been quiet until now. "Hijab, hijab, hijab! *Bo-ring!*" she declared, thrusting her shoulders back and crossing her arms. "I'm changing the topic. Tell me you don't want to know about Marcus and I'll tell you I have three heads."

I spun around on my heel.

"You're still going out with him? I thought your parents—"

Nafees cut me off. "Hmph. My parents!" she growled.

"I don't know…" Heba looked around at the rest of us. "Are we even allowed to talk about boyfriends during Ramadan?"

"I wouldn't lose sleep over it," Nafees said. "And anyway, it doesn't matter. He's history."

"What?" I couldn't believe my ears. "But…"

"You heard me. He's out of my life."

"How come?" I asked. "Did your father put his foot down?"

"Nah. Marcus turned out to be a total jerk, that's how come."

"Don't stop now. Go on!"

"I caught him red-handed at the laundromat with another girl. The two of them were making out right there next to the washing machines. When I yelled at him, he looked through me like I wasn't even there. But do I look like I care? No sir! She can have him because I don't want him. Bye-bye, Marcus!"

"You must be so bummed!" Amal said.

"Oh, don't worry about me," Nafees said breezily. "I'm fine."

"You do seem to have recovered rather nicely," Heba observed.

"What can I say? Life goes on," Nafees replied. "Boys! Who needs them?"

"Did you tell your parents?" Sehr asked.

"Do you think I'm nuts?" Nafees snorted.

"Was she really pretty? This other girl? Is that why he picked her?"

"I'm not wasting my time thinking about either one of them, but since you asked, she's uglier than a toad with knobby warts and probably dumber than a doorknob—and he's the biggest loser there ever was!"

It was hard for me to decide which news delivered the greater punch. Sehr's story had been disturbing, but Nafees's story had been, well, sort of thrilling.

Nafees didn't have a boyfriend anymore. She was back to square one, just like me.

I couldn't stop thinking about Josh, but I knew he wasn't thinking about me. When he wasn't playing basketball, he was hanging out with Juliana; when I saw them together on the court, my heart sank even further. How could I compete with that? I couldn't even toss a crumpled sheet of notebook paper into the wastebasket without missing by a mile. To make things worse, Josh was running for student council president and Juliana for fifth-grade homeroom rep. Now the campaign would throw them together even more.

"Josh would make a great president," I told Winnie. "I'd campaign for him in a snap if he asked me."

"He probably doesn't need any help."

"Everybody needs help," I said. "I'd need help if I ran for office."

"Would you? Run, I mean?" Winnie asked.

"Not in a million years."

"I'd be your campaign manager," Winnie said. "I'd help you win."

"Run for president? Are you out of your mind?"

"What about secretary, or homeroom rep?"

"No thanks."

"I mean it. You should run against Juliana."

"Why? So I can make a fool of myself?" I asked. "Juliana is hugely popular. I'd get crushed like a bug."

"Not true. She only hangs out with Nicole and Morgan," Winnie said. "Haven't you noticed?"

"That's only because she doesn't bother to talk to anyone else."

"Exactly. And if you don't take the time to talk to others, then how can you make friends with them?" Winnie asked.

"What's your point?"

"My point is you should run for our class rep too. You'd definitely have my support."

"Why don't *you* run?" I asked. "You'd get lots of votes."

"Nah," Winnie said. "Politics don't interest me. I'd make a great campaign manager, though!"

"I don't know, Winnie…"

"Just think," Winnie said. "If you won, you'd get to spend more time with Josh. Then he'd notice you for sure. One hundred percent guaranteed!"

Wednesday, November 20
6:00 p.m.

Dear Allah,

Today's fast was fine. As usual, Amma went overboard with my iftar.

While I was saying my evening prayer, Winnie's words kept popping into my mind and I couldn't really focus on You. Sorry.

I thought about what she said all the way home. Maybe I should take a risk, like Winnie says. But the thought of running against Juliana is scarier than that pause at the top just before the steep plunge on the Rocky Roads Roller Coaster. It's the part that Zayd loves the most, but I hate it. I really do! He always says that no one is forcing me to go on the roller coaster, but how can you go to an amusement park and not go on the roller coaster? Zayd tells me to close my eyes and keep them shut for the whole ride, but it works better for me to keep them wide open and scream at the top of my lungs all the way down. When the ride is over, my throat is sore but I have survived. I'm too chicken to hold my hands up like he does, though.

Lately, I've been feeling that I need a makeover, like the ones you see on TV. Ever since I saw M lay into Austin, I have thought about it. I'm getting tired of sweaty palms. I am! I want to be fearless like Winnie and Amal and Nafees, and…most of all like M.

Yours truly,

A

PS I'm taking a little break from fasting tomorrow. I told Amma I felt kind of woozy, and she got all worried and said I should skip a day or two to get my strength back for school. I hope You don't mind terribly. I'll start up again real soon, I promise.

"I'm thinking about running for my homeroom rep," I said at dinner.

"That's great, Aliya," Baba said. "Getting involved is so

much better than standing on the sideline."

"We need more of our young people getting involved in politics," Mom said. "We need bright kids speaking up for us."

"Mom, it's only grade school." I didn't quite see how the Glen Meadow Student Council was going to solve the problems of American Muslims. All the council did was stuff like fund-raisers and spirit days.

"It doesn't matter that it's just school," she said. "The important thing is that your voice would be heard, no matter how big or small the issue."

"Yes, yes, you should do it," Badi Amma said after Amma explained everything to her. "When I was your age, I was captain of the basketball team."

"You played basketball?" Zayd asked.

"Yes." Badi Amma laughed. "And I was such a tall thing, everyone said, 'Oh oh! All is lost! *Lumbu* has the ball, *Lumbu* has the ball!'"

"What's lumbu?" Zayd asked.

"Tall person," Badi Amma explained. "It is Urdu for tall person."

"But you were in high school then, Badi Amma," I said. "You told me last time."

"It doesn't matter, the age. But it matters that I was captain and I threw the ball in the hoop."

"Yes, Badi Amma," Baba said, looking at my great-grandmother with a big grin. "You are absolutely right!"

"She certainly is." Mom turned to me. "Age doesn't

matter and the issue doesn't matter either. What *does* matter is that you put yourself right in the middle of things with your head held high."

"Yes, yes," Badi Amma agreed.

Then my mother told me about Iqbal Massih, a Pakistani kid who spoke out against child slavery, and about an eighteen-year-old who got elected mayor somewhere in this country. I think she was trying to inspire me.

But more than anything, I wanted to feel good about myself around Juliana.

Marwa

I think I'll do it," I told Winnie on the way to homeroom. "I'm going to run for class rep."

"Great! I'll start working on our campaign plans right away," she said. "Juliana had better watch out."

"It would be so great to beat her."

Winnie gave me a sly look. "I like this new you a lot. I bet Josh will too."

I grinned. Running for class rep was sounding better and better. "I'll ask Mom to buy poster board for our signs."

"Fluorescent," Winnie said. "And I'll think up some great slogans. We're going to beat the pants off Juliana."

"Woo hoo!" I shouted.

Mrs. Doyle kept us pretty busy all morning. We had to write definitions of difficult words and include textual evidence in our literary responses. I was so focused on my work, I didn't fully catch the message when Mrs. Holmes's voice boomed over the intercom.

"What did she say?" I asked Winnie.

Winnie giggled. "The boys' bathroom is off limits!"

"He's done it again!" I said.

"Who's done what again?"

"It's Austin. He doesn't give up, does he?"

"How can you be sure it's him? It could be anyone."

"It's definitely Austin," I insisted. "Only he is mean enough to do this."

"Shh!" Juliana hissed. "Some of us are trying to work."

I clamped my mouth shut, but I was pretty sure she had overheard our conversation.

"I hear *someone*'s going for class rep," Juliana sneered as we left the cafeteria after lunch.

"Aliya can run against you if she wants to," Winnie said. "The last time I checked, this was still the home of the free and the land of the brave. I'd say you've got plenty to worry about!"

"Do I look the teeniest bit worried? But who said anything about her anyway? I was talking about Maar-waah." Juliana extended Marwa's name so far I was sure it'd snap.

"What could she be thinking?" Nicole piped up.

Marwa was running for student council? The new girl? The girl in hijab? That was pretty unbelievable.

"She's never going to win, not in a million years," Juliana scoffed.

Nicole rolled her eyes. "I'd never vote for her if I were in her homeroom."

"Me neither," said Morgan.

"Come on," Juliana said to Morgan and Nicole. "Let's go see what you-know-who thinks about all this." They turned on their heels and walked away. I thought they were going to talk to Josh, but they headed toward Austin, who was chucking stones at the chain-link fence. My heart sank.

"Oh, by the way," Juliana called back over her shoulder. "Good luck with your campaign, Aliya. You'll need it."

"Not as much as you!" I shouted.

"Atta girl!" urged Winnie. "You tell her!"

But that didn't help much. Juliana's smirks were bad enough. Now it appeared I was headed for trouble once Juliana finished tattling to Austin.

Suddenly I didn't want to be bothered with any of it.

"I don't know, Winnie. Maybe I shouldn't run after all," I said.

"Excuse me? You can't be getting all wishy-washy on me!" Winnie cried. "You've got to stick to your commitment."

"I didn't commit. I said I was thinking about it."

"I'm not going to forgive you if you chicken out now," Winnie said. "I've already made a list of plans I was going to discuss with you."

Austin cornered me before the bell sounded.

"Hey, you! Alien! Think you can escape?"

"My name is Aliya, not Alien," I said with my heart in my mouth.

"Aliya…alien. Same difference," he growled. "You're probably illegal too!"

"I am not! Why don't you just leave me alone? What did I ever do to you?"

"Spread lies, that's what!"

"What kind of lies? I don't know what you're talking about." I didn't like the way this was going.

"Did you, or did you not say I backed up the toilets?"

My mouth went dry. Juliana had squealed. I clenched both my fists. "I…"

Austin stepped closer. "You are dead meat!" he snarled.

"I'll tell the teacher if you threaten me," I said backing away.

"Oooh, scary," he snorted. "Look at me. I'm shaking in my boots."

I turned and walked quickly toward the other side of the school yard.

"Yeah! Run and hide, chicken!" he yelled. "Alien!"

As I darted by the picnic bench, Marwa called out, "Aliya, are you okay? You seem sort of—"

"I'm fine," I replied, mostly to convince myself. I looked around to make sure Austin wasn't following me.

"Are you fasting today?" she asked.

"I'm taking a little break now. I'll start up again pretty soon. Are you?"

"Yes. Al humdu lillah."

"How do you do it?" I asked.

"What do you mean?"

"I mean, you always seem so calm. Don't you ever get hungry?"

"Sure, I get hungry," she said. "But I try not to think about it. Plus, it's easier when you're busy. It helps to keep your mind off it." Some of her hair peeked out from under her hijab, which matched her hazel eyes perfectly.

"Your hair's a pretty color," I said, sitting down next to her. "Almost golden. I hadn't noticed before." I looked at the book she was reading. There was a picture of a young girl on the cover: blonde hair, side ponytails, bangs, defiant face. "What are you reading?"

"It's something Sarah recommended. *The Great Gilly Hopkins*."

"You like it?"

"It's actually a pretty good book. I really like the main character, Gilly."

"What's so great about her?"

"I'm just beginning to find out," Marwa said. "She seems to have a lot of spunk. You know, sort of brash and fearless."

That sounded like Winnie and Nafees. "Tell me more about her." I really wanted to know. I could use some spunk.

"She has a tough life and she has to struggle to deal with everything. She's pretty hard to get along with."

"She doesn't sound all that likeable to me."

"Well, she isn't at first. But her family situation explains a lot of her behavior. Her mother doesn't want her and so Gilly is sent to different foster homes. She acts up all the time and has a terrible attitude. Consequently, nobody else wants her either. But then she's sent to live with this lady called Trotter who has a big heart but is generally a slob."

"I'd hate it if my mom didn't want me," I said.

"Talk about problems, huh?"

"Is there a happy ending?" I asked.

"I haven't got to the end yet, but I'm predicting there is," Marwa said. "I have a feeling Gilly is going to learn to make the best of the situation and channel her anger in the right direction. At least that's what I hope happens."

"She sounds interesting." I sighed. "She doesn't sound like someone stuck in a hole."

"Stuck in a hole?"

"You know…when someone feels sorry for herself and wallows and cries 'Poor me, poor me' all the time?"

"Hmm. I don't think so. This girl strikes me as a fighter, not a wallower."

I stared at her. She always sounded so grown-up. "Are you sure you're a kid? How old are you anyway?"

Marwa smiled. "When I was little, I was very sick and lost a year of school. That makes me one year older than you."

She was the same age as Amal and Nafees. But she was so much more serious than Amal and a lot more mature than Nafees. I looked into her face again, at her eyes and at the birthmark near her lips.

"You're doing it again," Marwa said. "Are you seeing something that shouldn't be there?"

I shook my head. "Nah. It's all good."

Marwa snapped her book shut. "Let's walk around for a while," she said. "I need to stretch my legs."

"You shouldn't strain yourself too much since you're fasting," I cautioned.

"Don't worry. It'll be fine," she said.

We walked past the playground equipment and headed for the basketball courts.

"Where's Winnie?" Marwa asked.

"She's out sick today."

"You're best friends, aren't you?"

I was surprised she knew that. Had she being paying attention to me when I was doing my best to avoid her? "Yeah. I've known her forever."

"You must talk about everything," she said. "That happens when you're best friends, right?"

I thought about that. Winnie and I talked about a lot of things but not about everything. For instance, I hadn't told her I wished Marwa hadn't come to Glen Meadow. Winnie wouldn't have understood, plus she would've asked a ton of questions.

"Yeah, mostly," I replied. "Do you have someone to talk to?"

"My dad and I have all kinds of interesting talks."

"I meant a kid," I said.

"I have friends. But a best friend? Not yet. Maybe soon."

We stopped at the Bradford pear. In early spring, it resembled a giant snow cone. Now it was surrounded by dead leaves. I kicked them up and watched them rain back down. We watched Austin throwing rocks at the fence on the other side of the schoolyard.

"That's one angry kid," Marwa said.

"And a pretty weird one. Do you think he has problems at home? Like Gilly?"

"Who knows?" she said. "I saw him talking with you earlier. Was he saying mean stuff?"

I shrugged.

"He's said mean things to me too." Her voice was quiet but firm.

"He has?"

"It started after the apple incident," she said. "Until then, I was just a strange bug for him to stare at."

"What's he been saying?"

"He says that outsiders should stay out of his country's politics."

She said it as though it was a funny joke but it was not. *It's because of your hijab*, I wanted to say. But instead I asked her how she had handled it.

"I had to think about it a little," Marwa said.

"And?"

"And…I asked him to vote for me in the election."

"Oh, wow. What did he say?"

"Nothing. He was too shocked that I'd spoken to him. I told him I'd noticed that the other kids always listened to him. I said I probably wouldn't win without his vote."

"But his vote isn't going to help you win the election."

"I know that, but he doesn't."

"That's pretty sneaky," I said.

"What's wrong with making someone feel good?" Marwa replied. "It's only a teeny white lie and it's not hurting anyone."

"Did you also get *that* from your dad?" I asked. "Anyway, what did Austin do?"

"He gave this yeah-right! snort and left."

"I can't believe you're running for class rep, though!" I blurted out. There, I'd said it.

"You can't?"

"I mean, you just got here. You probably don't even know all the kids yet. How can you be sure they'll vote for you?"

Marwa shrugged. "I *don't* know if they'll vote for me."

"Well?"

"But I hope they will."

"Aren't you afraid you'll lose?" I asked.

"My dad says one never thinks of loss until it happens and then one deals with it. And anyway, if I lose…" She shrugged and went on. "I'll never know unless I try, right?"

I found myself wanting to protect her from the hurt she was bound to feel when she lost the election. "Maybe you should've waited until next year to run for office."

Marwa shook her head. "My dad says there's no time

like the present. He says the present's the only moment we can control."

The bell sounded and we walked back to the building. Marwa's words replayed in my head the whole way in. She hadn't sounded at all wishy-washy. She had sounded like a person whose mind was made up. Period.

"Well, good luck," I said, giving her a thumbs-up. It seemed the right thing to do.

"Thanks," she said. "Good luck to you too."

Choti Dahdi

He called you a *what*?" Mom shouted, dropping her fork. The dinner table went silent.

"An alien," I repeated. "That's what he said."

"Alien sounds like Aliya," Zayd said. "She'd be a Martian if she were from Mars."

"Be quiet, Zayd," Amma snapped.

"See?" Mom said, turning to Baba.

"See what?" Baba asked.

"I can't believe how casual you are about this." Mom threw both her arms in the air. "Your daughter is bullied at school and you can sit there as placid and still as a pond?"

"People are afraid of what they don't understand, Aliya," Baba said. "They say and do stupid and—"

"And the innocent get hurt!" Mom interrupted, pointing at me. "It's the people who simply go about their daily lives who get to feel the brunt of their anger."

"Baba, could you talk to Mrs. Holmes about him?" I asked. "It's not just me anymore. Austin has said mean things to Marwa too." I told my parents what she had told me in the school yard.

"See? Now we are outsiders?" Mom said. "And this is coming from the mouth of babes? I want the flag out of the attic and on our front door *today*!"

"Why?" Zayd asked.

"So people will see it and know we are patriotic," Mom replied.

"If it makes you feel better." Baba smiled. "Are you climbing up there or do you want me to go?"

"What sort of question is that?" Mom said. "Do I look like an attic climber?"

"I pledge 'allegems' to the flag every day," my brother announced.

"You mean 'pledge of allegiance,' dork!" I corrected.

"Enough, both of you," said Baba. "Aliya, I'll make an appointment with Mrs. Holmes soon. I'm sure we can work this out somehow."

We ate in relative silence for a little while. Baba and Mom always used a fork, but Amma and Badi Amma ate with their fingers according to their tradition. They said all foods had their special eating utensil—there was the fork and knife for steak, chopsticks for shrimp lo mein, and fingers for rice and *dhal*.

Amma pushed all the spinach bits from the rim of Zayd's plate back on his rice with her finger, but he scraped it away again. "How will you be strong like Popeye if you don't eat your spinach?" Amma asked.

"I don't want to be strong like him," Zayd replied. "Aliya, who's Popeye anyway?"

"Aliya *Apa*," Badi Amma said sharply.

"Popeye is an ugly cartoon sailor with big muscles," I replied. "Don't you know anything?"

Right in the middle of dinner, the telephone rang.

"Probably one of those fund-raising calls," Baba said, but Mom was already up.

"It's Choti Dahdi!" she mouthed from the far end of the room.

"She should have let it ring," Zayd whispered.

Mom held the phone to her ear for a very long time. She finally told my great-grandaunt goodbye and hung up. "She's arriving the day after tomorrow!" she announced.

My brother and I looked at each other in dismay. We knew what that meant. Choti Dahdi would stay forever and turn everything upside down. I'd have to move out of my room into Zayd's. Mom would charge about like a windup toy, changing the sheets, washing towels, cleaning the bathtub and sink—all so Choti Dahdi wouldn't screech about damp smells and globs of toothpaste.

Choti Dadhi couldn't help it, Amma said. She was who she was: a little weird, a little annoying, and a lot snoopy, sticking her long nose where it didn't belong. *Did we pray five times a day? Did we eat halal food? When was I going to cover my head with the hijab? Why did my knees show under my dress?* Her teeth clicked when she chewed and she never said "excuse me" when she burped.

And she would be arriving just one week before Thanksgiving!

Mom took the news particularly hard. "What will I do about the turkey?" she cried.

Our Butterball was already in the freezer and the boxes of Pepperidge Farm stuffing and cans of Ocean Spray cranberry sauce had been purchased. The turkey was fine for us and for my aunts and uncles and their families who lived nearby. But Choti Dahdi only ate meat that was halal.

"She will eat the *pulao* and *baghare baigan* and *kut*… That will be enough for her," Badi Amma growled.

"It's the turkey that worries me," Mom said. "She'll hit the roof when she discovers it's not halal."

"We'll never hear the end of it!" Amma moaned.

"We could pretend the Butterball is halal," I suggested.

"Eh? Kya Bole?" asked Badi Amma, but Mom and Amma looked like I had just proposed robbing a bank.

I backpedaled quickly. "It's just an idea. Sorry."

"*Tauba, tauba!*" Amma said, striking her cheeks alternately with her hand, shaming me. She sounded like Choti Dahdi.

"I guess I'll go to Horowitz Kosher Meat Market and get a kosher turkey," Mom grumbled. "But turkeys never go on sale there." Kosher meat was something like halal meat, so she knew it would be acceptable to Choti Dahdi.

"Kya Bole?" Badi Amma cupped her hand to her ear.

"She's getting a kosher turkey!" Amma shouted.

"*Hanh?*"

Choti Dahdi was causing a big tizzy and she wasn't even here yet!

I packed up my clothes to take to Zayd's room while Mom gave mine the once-over.

"Why do I always have to move?" I grumbled. "Why can't she sleep in Zayd's room or the basement?"

"You know the answer to that, Aliya." Mom gave me her you're-pushing-my-limits look. "She's an old lady. Besides, she's a relative and a guest and we honor and respect our elders in this house."

I knew I couldn't win this fight, so I tried to show my annoyance in a different way. "You're so worried about the halal turkey. What's she going to eat before and after Thanksgiving?"

Mom flapped out a freshly laundered bed sheet and I grabbed it by its other end. Together we placed it on my bed and tucked in the corners.

"Indo/Pak Mart sells other meats and it's only ten minutes away," Mom said.

"You could get a halal turkey at Zabeeha Meats," I suggested.

"I am *not* driving fifty miles," Mom said in a voice that told me the discussion had ended.

Thursday, November 21
8:00 p.m.

Dear Allah,

I have officially lost my privacy. I moved into Zayd's room. I'm sleeping on his top bunk bed.

OCD (Get it? Old Choti Dahdi) is coming tomorrow. Zayd and I are going to have to be on our best behavior around her. Mom has warned us to be especially respectful. My prediction is Zayd and I will be saying a lot of Assalam alaikums around OCD. It's a good thing it's not summer. I couldn't wear shorts with her in the house.

I was hoping M wouldn't ask about the fast today, but she did. I told her I was taking a break for two or three days. I'll fast again on the weekend, just so OCD doesn't throw a fit.

Please, can You do something about her visits? She just pops in and stays on and on and Mom makes me give up my room. I'm not even allowed to complain about it. But I suppose sleeping in Zayd's room is a whole lot better than sleeping alone in a cold basement.

Austin called me an Alien. What an idiot! Baba's going to talk to Mrs. Holmes. I wish I could handle it on my own—I really do. But I don't exactly know how.

I'm running for homeroom rep. Winnie and I are starting our preparations for the campaign. Mom is going to buy the poster board. Amma has a lot of tape in the basement, along with the piles of used gift wrap she refuses to throw away.

I'll tell You a secret: the real reason I finally made up my mind to run was M. I was really, really surprised to hear that she was going for it. And she's being so casual about the whole thing. How does she do it? I wish I could be like that. But I'm also running because I want to beat Juliana.

Winnie says I can win; we just have to campaign really hard. I'm not afraid of hard work.

If I win, maybe Josh will be friendlier to me. I am hoping, anyway. I've decided I'm going to talk to him.

I sometimes imagine Josh kissing me on the lips!

I haven't told a soul. Not even Winnie!

Yours truly,

A

PS If I win, it will be fun to shout in Austin's face, "Who's the loser now?"

Choroughly Mixed Up

The Bismillah sign on your door still loose! When in Allah's name are you fixing?" Choti Dadhi demanded as soon as she stepped in the door before she even wished us her usual "Assalam alaikum."

She was skinny like spaghetti and bent over like a fish-hook. Her hijab came to a peak over her forehead, and a long tooth hung over her bottom lip like Strega Nona's in the picture books. She clutched a walking cane in one hand and her prayer beads in the other. They were the biggest and shiniest crystals I had ever seen.

Badi Amma and OCD hugged each other. Then Zayd and I stepped forward, cupping our right hands to our foreheads to pay our respects and wish her peace.

"*Adab*, Choti Dahdi."

"Assalam alaikum, Choti Dahdi."

OCD returned our greetings solemnly. She pinched my chin with her fingertips, raised them to her own lips, and kissed them with a big smack: *um-mah*! Then she turned to my mother and said, "Your daughter become fat, fat. What you feeding, hanh?"

"What about you, Choti Dahdi?" Mom asked, trying to change the subject. "Are you hungry?"

"Not exactly. But we would eat 'eespesheel K' with banana slice and one percent milk." She sat down at the table and waited for Mom to serve her. "The 'sekeerity' rang—bhaanh-bhaanh—for us in 'Minnipolice' airport," she went on. "We told 'sekeerity' guard not to worry: It's the ujjad metal in our knee!"

Zayd and I exchanged quick glances. Ujjad meant 'horrible' or 'bad' and we braced ourselves to hear it used a zillion times during Choti Dahdi's visit.

Like it or not, our Choti Dahdi was here to stay.

On Saturday morning, OCD joined Mom, Amma, and me for suhur. Amma heaped scrambled eggs on my plate and told me not to leave a bite.

OCD's tongue clicked in her mouth as she ate her cereal. "You have poor attitude about Ramadan one year ago, hmm?" she said. "Do you remember this?"

I shook my head.

"We fix you!" she said gleefully.

"How so?" asked Amma.

"With a nice, nice talk. Aliya say going without food and water for thirty days too hard," OCD elaborated. "We ask her, 'What is suhur for but to sustain you?' We remind and remind that fasting is one of the five important practices of

Islam and a solemn duty for Muslim." She looked over at me. "Do you remember we say this, hanh?"

I had no memory of this lecture, but I was too sleepy to argue.

"She was just a little kid, *Khala*," Amma said, using the Urdu term for maternal aunt.

"Aii! She not so little. She quite big enough to keep good attitude about important matters of religion," OCD said, slurping her milk.

Amma rushed us to finish. "Eat up, eat up," she said. "Suhur time is almost ending."

"When is she going to wear hijab, hanh?" OCD asked.

I looked up in alarm.

"We're not going to talk about that now!" Amma cleared away the empty plates with an angry flourish. "Aliya, hurry and say your prayers before the sun rises."

"Just asking," OCD sniffed. "Why getting snippety?"

I spread out the prayer mat on the floor and performed the prayer.

"*Aii!* Prayer rug not pointing to Kaaba exactly," I heard her mutter.

I bet you ten dollars Allah won't mind, I said to myself.

Thanksgiving

After days of fasting from dawn to dusk, Thanksgiving finally arrived. OCD had settled in comfortably and our house was good and ready for a feast, right in the middle of Ramadan. Zayd said this year Thanksgiving was going to be like the prize in the Happy Meal Ramadan box and for once I agreed with him.

On Thanksgiving Day, I was too excited to go back to sleep after suhur. I lay in the top bunk in Zayd's room and waited for daylight. OCD was back in my bed already; I could hear her snoring from across the hall.

I must have dozed off because when I woke up again, the wonderful fragrances of Thanksgiving filled the house. I could smell cinnamon from the pies and rosemary and thyme from the stuffing, and over that, the other exotic aromas of Amma's old family recipes.

Mom and Amma had cooked up a feast. There was lamb *biryani* and chicken *khorma* and baghare baigan along with cranberry sauce, mashed potatoes, corn, and peas. The main dishes—the Butterball and kosher turkeys—were ready for the oven. The countertops were spotless, the sink gleamed like silver, and the whole house was spic and span. A bouquet of fall flowers sat on the table.

My mother fussed around the two birds, each sitting proudly in its own foil pan. "This one is kosher, right?" she asked Amma.

"Hmm…I think so…but it looks exactly like that one." Amma pondered the turkeys. "Let's be sure, shall we?"

My genius grandmother wrapped a red twist tie around the leg of Choti Dahdi's turkey.

"That's good," Mom said. "Better to be safe now than sorry later!"

I examined them closely. "It's good they're the same size. They'll look nice and symmetrical on the table."

Amma started the stuffing on the stove top and Mom opened the cans of cranberry sauce.

"Mom, did you put garlic and ginger in the turkey?" I asked.

"Yes," she replied. "And loads of *Shaan Charga* spices."

Amma counted back the hours from iftar by touching the spaces on her fingers with her thumb. "We will put the turkeys in the oven at 12:30," she declared.

"Is a kosher turkey the same as a halal turkey?" I asked.

"Not technically," Mom replied. "But it's close enough."

"Why didn't you just get a halal turkey?"

"I told you already," Mom said. "For one thing, I didn't want to drive sixty miles."

"You said it was fifty miles," I said.

My brother jumped in. "What's the other thing?" he asked.

"You ask far too many questions!" Mom snapped. "You two run on and straighten up your room! Go!"

The house gradually filled with noisy relatives. Baba's sister and her husband, who lived in a nearby town, brought their two rowdy boys. Mom's brother and his wife drove up a bit later, their two kids in tow. Baba's cousin and her family, who lived the farthest away, arrived last.

Relationships in my family are clearly defined. A *Mamu* is an uncle, but only if he's your Mom's brother. A *Phupu* is an aunt but only if she's your father's sister. Your mother's sister is a Khala, never a Phupu. And your father's brother is your *Chacha*, and cannot be your Mamu.

The air was heavy with Charga spice and soon the real smells of Thanksgiving were completely masked. I helped my grandmother spread our geometric *dusterkhan* cloth on the floor of the family room, where the kids would eat.

When the oven timer buzzed at last, Amma jiggled the drumsticks and said that the turkey twins were done. Mom asked Baba to take care of them while she got dressed.

A short time later, we heard him yell, "Honey, they're ready!" About two minutes after that, Mom shrieked. Zayd and I came running.

Two identical birds sat side by side on ceramic platters.

Mom was standing in front of them, staring. "Where's the twisty tie?" she demanded.

Baba looked perplexed. "I threw it out. I thought you'd want me to."

"Now what am I going to do?" Mom moaned. "Just get out of the kitchen. Leave! I need to figure out this mess on my own!"

Baba beat a hasty retreat with a quizzical look on his face and turkey grease down the front of his shirt.

"Why didn't you say something?" Mom asked me.

"I was in Badi Amma's room," I said. "Honest!"

Mom frowned and poked at the turkey on the left. "Is it this one?

"It could be...," Amma replied.

"Or is it that one?"

My grandmother held her finger up to her lips and gave my mother a wink. After a moment, Mom nodded, and they both went about their business as if everything was just fine.

OCD wandered in. "Aii! You cooked *two, two!*" she exclaimed, peering closely. "Halal?"

"Kosher," Amma replied without batting an eyelid.

"Aii, what happened to halal?" OCD asked petulantly. She prodded the turkeys with a bony finger. "*Our* halal turkeys very famous in *Minnipolice*," she muttered. "So succulent, so flavorful you *vhant* to suck on bone, sinew, *and* gristle."

❖

The setting sun told us it was time for iftar. First Mom served plump dates so we could ceremoniously break our fast before we moved to our Thanksgiving meal. When we were done, Baba carried the steaming platters into the dining room and my aunts made room for the biryani and khorma and kebabs on our big table.

"Vhait! No dinner until evening prayers are performed!" yelled OCD.

We made our ablutions, spread our prayer mats in the family room, and lined up in neat rows behind Baba. He touched his thumbs to his earlobes and made the call to prayer. Together, we recited verses from the Holy Quran and praises to Allah. Together, we asked for His blessings. Prayer performed and mats folded away, we hurried to our long-awaited Thanksgiving-in-Ramadan dinner.

Suddenly OCD held up her hand. "Aii!" she cried, staring pointedly at Baba. "Forgetting again, hanh?"

My father cleared his throat and rapped on the table with his fork.

OCD jumped in to help. "No talking, no talking!" she shouted.

"O Allah, we thank you for the gift of food, faith, and family," Baba said.

Happily, this was a much shorter prayer. *"Ameen,"* we answered loudly.

After that, it was a free-for-all. The kids piled mountains of food on their plates and sat cross-legged around the dusterkhan, eating the stuffing with forks and the biryani with their fingers. The grown-ups crowded around the table; hands and elbows bumped as the food was passed.

"Choti Dahdi, you must use a knife to cut the meat," Zayd called.

"Aii!" OCD curved a finger under her nostril to express her puzzlement. "Allah gave us fingers and teeth and, Masha' Allah, we still have all of ours, see?" She bared her teeth at my brother and then returned to gnawing at her turkey.

Who got the Butterball and who ate the kosher turkey that day was anybody's guess. Allah knew, of course, because He is all knowing. But He is also all forgiving…that is what Badi Amma says.

Thanksgiving
Thursday, November 28
9:00 p.m.

Dear Allah,

All the relatives have left but OCD, and it's pretty quiet in the house now. It was a great Thanksgiving, except for the mix-up over the turkeys.

Is it very bad if OCD did eat the wrong turkey? She thought she was eating a kosher turkey, which would be all right, so did it really matter that it wasn't halal? It's sort of confusing to me.

Either way, I wish someone would take OCD down a notch or two. She makes me ask permission to enter my own room! And she's always sending me on errands to get things for her.

Yours truly,

A

PS Never mind. I think I see the point now. Mom probably should have served a halal turkey.

Nafees called the following day. "I'm reeeally bored," she drawled. "Tell your mom to call mine up and invite me over?"

"I can't," I said. "Winnie's coming over so we can catch up on our independent study project."

"Didn't anybody tell you? You're not supposed to do schoolwork during Thanksgiving break."

"Ha ha, very funny. And I'm also behind on Sister Khan's project."

"Don't remind me!" Nafees groaned. "I haven't even started mine yet."

I heard the doorbell. "Oops, sorry," I said. "Winnie's here. Gotta go."

Winnie went straight to my great-grandmother's room. "Hi, Buddy Ma," she called from the door.

Badi Amma was in bed, propped up by two pillows. The TV was blaring and she was watching the screen intently.

"BUDDY MA, HI!" Winnie called again at the top of her voice.

My great-grandmother turned. "Little Veenee, *tum kub aye?*"

"What?" Winnie looked at me. "What did she just say?"

"She asked when you came," I explained.

"How do I answer in Urdu?" Winnie asked, and I told her.

"BUDDY MA, *MAI ABHI AYEE!*"

"Oh, just now? Good, very good. Glad to see you. Go in kitchen and eat something. Eat a lot. Don't mind the rest. They are fasting. It is Ramadan, you know, Little Vinnee?"

"Okay, Buddy Ma," Winnie said with a grin. "Bye."

We took a detour through the kitchen and Winnie grabbed a samosa. "Aren't you going to eat one?" she asked. "They're delicious."

"I'm fasting today," I reminded her.

"Sorry. I can't keep track anymore. Isn't the torture over yet?"

"Shhh, OCD will hear you," I said.

"I thought she didn't speak much English."

"She understands more than she lets on," I said.

We almost collided with my great-aunt in the hallway upstairs. She had just awakened from her afternoon nap in my bed and there was a big scowl on her face. Her prayer beads dangled from her hand.

"What's the matter, Choti Dahdi?" I asked.

"Uff! That ujjad mattress gave us a horrid backache again," she moaned with one hand on the small of her back. She looked at Winnie. "Hello?"

"Um, this is my friend and she's helping me with my project." I spoke hurriedly. I didn't want OCD to embarrass me further.

"What you name?"

"Excuse me?" asked Winnie. "Oh, sorry. MY NAME IS WINNIE!"

"Aii!" OCD turned to me. "Why this mad girl shouting?"

"Winnie," I muttered under my breath. "Choti Dadhi isn't deaf!"

"Oops," Winnie said. "I was thinking about Buddy Ma." She pointed to my great-grandaunt's hand. "Cool beads! Are they real?"

"What this girl say?" OCD asked me and I translated for her.

She smiled broadly at Winnie, swinging her luminous crystal beads. "Yes, yes, very *gooood*. Pay a *laaat* money."

A Walking-Talking Tent

Fasting?" I asked, sitting down across from Marwa on
the picnic bench.

"Al humdu lillah," she said. "And you?"

"Al humdu lillah," I replied, smiling at our little ritual.
"Only one more day to go." It was hard to believe that the
whole month of Ramadan had gone by. Somewhere along
the way I had begun to feel stronger inside. It had happened
very quietly and smoothly, but I could tell. Each new fast
day seemed less burdensome, and pretty soon even the
campaign jitters had faded. "You fasted a lot. It seemed
every time I turned around, you weren't eating."

"Al humdu lillah," she repeated. "I did as many as I
could."

I smiled. I had a feeling that Marwa, unlike me, must
have already started her period. Women and girls were
excused from fasting during their time of the month but I
wondered if she'd skipped some days because she hadn't
felt well.

"We did it, and it feels good, right?" she added.

I didn't have to think too long about that. Yes, it felt very, very good. "I guess a person can do pretty much anything once she puts her mind to it."

"No matter how big or small that thing is," Marwa said.

Our breath steamed in the cold December air.

"Where's Winnie?" Marwa asked.

"She's probably hanging out with Leah, Madison, and Carly."

"You two have known each other for a long time, right?"

"Since kindergarten," I said.

"Yeah, it shows."

"It does? How?"

"Well…you seem happy to be with her and she is happy to be with you."

"Yeah. She's my best friend," I said.

The sound of kids at play surrounded us. I heard the swings creak and balls bounce.

"I haven't found a best friend yet," Marwa said quietly.

She was staring into space. I wanted to say something— something that sounded like an apology. I could have been the person to make her feel the way Winnie and I felt about each other. I could have made her feel more welcome.

I took a deep breath. "You've only just got here. It seems like you're pretty good friends with Sarah and Maggie."

Marwa nodded. "They're nice."

I threw my head back and let my hair hang behind me. It was past my shoulders now, and getting longer. I looked up at the winter sky, silent and pale blue with puffy white clouds.

"I miss the birds in the winter," I said. "Sometimes, you get lucky and see a whole flock of geese fly by, honking their heads off."

"It's great being outside like this, even when it's so cold," Marwa said. "I like to go hiking, especially near the water. I like lakes and rivers and oceans, but mostly I like lakes."

"There's a lake near our house. With lots of walking trails."

Some boys ran by, whooping and laughing. I could see Austin across the playground, standing by himself.

"What was it like in Morocco?" I asked.

"Morocco? I was seven when we left. We go back now and then. Sometimes I think about the courtyards and the *souks*—those are the marketplaces, always crowded and very noisy. But my favorite memories are the sound of the *adan*, the call to prayer from the minarets, and the smell of mint tea."

"Is it colorful?"

"Colorful?"

"My grandmother says India is colorful. I wouldn't know since I've been there only once, when I was very little."

"I don't remember a whole lot of color in Morocco. I'd like to go to India some day, though," Marwa said.

"And I'd like to visit Morocco."

Across the yard Mr. Gallagher was checking his watch. Recess was probably ending soon.

"I've been meaning to ask you something," I said.

"Oh?"

"How come you're not...um...I mean, you never seem to be...um...embarrassed, you know..."

"Are you talking about my hijab?"

I nodded. "What else?"

"Oh, I don't know. You could be talking about anything, about my grades or my smelly lunch...?"

I laughed. "Well, it sure couldn't be your grades," I said. "You're waaay too smart."

"Why should I be embarrassed about the hijab? I mean, it's who I am, and I'm pretty okay with myself. It's a part of me."

"I don't know what you mean," I said.

"It's hard to explain. It's a feeling."

"I think I get it. Sort of like a zebra?"

"A zebra?" she asked.

"You know, the way a zebra feels with his stripes?"

"Exactly!" Marwa grinned. "I feel natural in it. My parents say I look really good. I like wearing it. I really do."

"It's your special stripe," I said.

"Yes, I guess that's what it is."

"You always seem so...so sure," I sighed. "I wish I could think like you."

"Who's stopping you?"

I didn't have an answer to her question so I didn't reply.

Austin tossed small twigs in the air and whacked them with a long stick. "Just look at that jerk," I said.

Marwa turned to look. "He called my mother a walking,

talking tent this morning. He even laughed at his own stupid joke."

My heart sank. *This is exactly why I didn't want a hijab at Glen Meadow in the first place,* I thought. *It screams out, "Look how different I am!"*

"That's not a joke," I told Marwa. "It's mean and hurtful and he's not going to get away with it. My dad's going to see to it."

She gave a little nod, staring straight ahead.

I couldn't see her eyes, but I knew what she was feeling. I thought about the woman who'd yelled at my mom. My eyes teared a little. Maybe it was just the cold air.

"I've been here forever and he still can't say my name right," I said, trying to cheer her up.

She laughed. "He says I should go home to I-*ran* and I-*raq* with the rest of the terrorists."

"That's not funny!" I said. "I don't see how you can laugh."

"It's not that," Marwa said. "It's just that I am from Morocco and Morocco is so far away from Iran and Iraq."

"So he doesn't know his geography either. You should still tell on him!"

Marwa shook her head. "Sometimes things like this will go away if we don't make a big fuss."

"Who told you that?" I asked. "It doesn't make any sense."

"My dad," she said.

I couldn't understand how she could be so calm. But I did understand the hurt.

"You know, this is the first time we've really talked since I came," Marwa said.

"You're wrong," I corrected her. "It's actually the second time."

"And it always seems to be about him," she said, waving a thumb in Austin's direction.

"Yeah!" I said. "We do have that moron in common."

"We have a lot more in common than that," Marwa said with a smile. "Eid too. Eid's the day after tomorrow."

"I know," I said. "I can't wait."

"We'll be wishing each other *Eid Mubrook* pretty soon," she said.

I nodded. "And you wished me Ramadan Mubrook not too long ago, do you remember?"

"Of course, I do!" she said. "You weren't as talkative back then."

The bell sounded and we took our time walking back. I was sorry that recess had ended.

December 3
9:00 p.m.

Dear Allah,

I can't wait for Eid! And Marwa was right—it is a pretty good feeling to know I made it through Ramadan! I was afraid that if she asked me how many days I'd fasted, I'd be embarrassed to tell her. But now I'm thinking there's no reason to be embarrassed. Eighteen days

may not be as good as twenty-nine or thirty, but it's better than six or seven or even my eight of last year.

I hardly think about her hijab now, except when I
wonder how she can tie it on so perfectly. It stays in place
all day and she always looks so nice. My scarf always
slides off when I bend down to say my prayer at the
Islamic Center. It's no use asking Mom what to do; she's
not much better at tying it than I am.

Marwa likes the outdoors too. It'll be fun to walk the
trails around the lake with her next summer.

Yours truly,

A

PS Marwa reminded me that I wasn't very friendly earlier.
I didn't know how to answer.

PPS It makes sense to me now that a hijab can be a part of
a person. Anyway, what's in our head is more important
than what's on it. Right?

Eid

The excitement and mad rush started pretty early in our house on the morning of Eid.

"OCD's hogging the bathroom again," I muttered. "She's been in there almost an hour."

"Do you think she's sleeping in the bathtub?" Zayd whispered.

"Mom will be mad that we're still in our pajamas." I put my ear to the door, trying to figure out what our great-grandaunt was still doing in there. "I'm going to knock."

"Is she snoring?"

I knocked on the bathroom door. "Choti Dahdi! May we have our turn, please?"

The toilet flushed and OCD opened the door. "Aii!" she said, looking down at me crossly. "You *vhant* break the door?"

"It's my turn." I squeezed past her.

Back in Zayd's room, I slipped quickly into my new green shalvar khameez with pink and blue trim. Zayd put on a pale gold brocade *shervani* and white *churidar* pajamas. He had combed his hair down severely; he actually looked cute.

"Where's the darn shoe polish?" Baba growled.

"We're going to be late for prayers at this rate!" Mom scolded him as she rushed down the hall.

OCD emerged from her room dressed in a long abbayah, her prayer beads spinning in her fingers.

"You look very glamorous, Choti Dahdi," I said.

She looked puzzled until Zayd explained that "glamorous" was a compliment. "You look very nice," he told her.

"Thank *Ooo!*" she said, grinning. "Thank *Ooo!*"

Finally, we were all ready. We threw our winter coats over our splendid Eid attire, piled into the van, waved to Amma and Badi Amma, and headed for the mosque. I felt a little sad that they weren't coming with us. My great-grandmother was getting too old to be out in the cold and my grandmother was staying with her.

We arrived at the Islamic Center with only fifteen minutes left to spare. The parking lot was overflowing, so we had to park on the street and walk a long way in the snow. The lobby was so jam-packed, there was hardly an inch left to maneuver, and the prayer hall was filling up really fast. We removed our shoes and hurried to find good spots.

Baba walked to the front with Zayd. OCD had me firmly by my arm. By chance I spotted Marwa in a far corner. Her eyes locked on mine. "Eid Mubarak," I mouthed across the sea of heads and Marwa waved back. But OCD's grip was like a vise and there was nothing I could do but follow as we searched for a place to sit. We found a spot and quickly made a dash for it.

Everybody in the prayer hall began chanting the preliminary adoration. This was the part that always gave me goose bumps. The entire hall resonated as we said the words in unison.

Allahu Akbar, Allahu Akbar, Allahu Akbar
La illaha il Allah
Allahu Akbar, Allahu Akbar
Walilahil Hamd

We praised Allah, the Great—all together, with one voice and one feeling. At the stroke of nine, the Imam stood and made the call to prayer. The congregation stood, creating a rolling, muffled rumble.

We all stood shoulder to shoulder in straight rows, waiting for our Imam to lead us into the Eid prayer. I looked around at all the women and girls dressed in their finery. My dupatta slipped from my head again and again. Choti Dahdi pulled it roughly back in place each time, hissing, "Hair is showing, hair is showing. Tauba, tauba!" When I pulled away, she threw me an annoyed look.

After the short Eid prayer, the Imam delivered a long sermon. My mind drifted. I craned my neck to look for Marwa again, but Choti Dahdi gave me a jab with her sharp elbow. When the Imam finished, shouts of "Eid Mubarak! Eid Mubarak!" erupted from the audience.

Everyone hugged, shook hands, and thumped each other on the backs. There was a lot of joy in the room.

Baba pushed his way through the crowd, tugging Zayd along. "Eid Mubarak, family!" He beamed and threw his arms around us.

We all returned the greeting: "Eid Mubarak!"

I saw Nafees, Ama, Heba, and Sehr huddled together near the doorway. I waved and they motioned me over.

"Where are you going?" Mom asked.

"I'll be right back, I promise," I said and fought my way through to my friends. The crowd pressed around me and I didn't see Marwa again. I was disappointed that I didn't get to wish her a happy Eid up close.

"You've got to hear what this one has to say," Amal said after we had exchanged Eid greetings.

"What is it, Nafees?" I asked.

"Not here." She looked up and down the hall furtively. "Let's go upstairs."

We ran up to our Religion 2 classroom, which was empty and silent. Nafees perched on top of a desk, itching to tell her news, and Amal and Heba and I gathered around to listen. Only Sehr lingered by the door, looking glum.

"What's wrong with you today, grumpy?" I asked her. "Smile. It's Eid, remember?"

Amal nudged me. "Haven't you heard?"

I looked at her blankly.

"She was minding her own business, walking—" Amal turned to Sehr. "Where were you, again?"

"I was actually in the mall, with my brother," Sehr said. "Some goon tried to pull off my hijab."

"Oh no!" I cried. "First your sister, now you! What did you do?"

"I wanted to chase him down and punch him in the face, but my brother stopped me."

"That's terrible!" I said. "Did you report it?"

"The mall security people just blew us off," Sehr said. "What do we have to be before they actually do something? Dead or something?"

"What about your parents?"

"They went to the police, but a fat lot of good that did! They actually made us feel we were making a big deal out of nothing."

"There really wasn't much the police could have done," Nafees pointed out. "Or anyone else, for that matter."

"Are you going to quit wearing it too, like your sister did?" I asked Sehr.

"I'm listening to my parents, I guess, and putting it away for a while until all this craziness goes away."

That made complete sense. I would have done the exact same thing. But Amal still wore her scarf all the time. My eyes went to her automatically.

"I know you're all thinking I'm a chicken for giving it up," Sehr said. "But believe me, when something like that happens to you, it's very scary."

"I wasn't thinking anything, honest," I said. And then I gave her a quick hug.

Nafees cleared her throat loudly. "Well, enough about scarves. Who's interested in hearing about something more exciting?"

"Oh right. This one has got herself a brand new boyfriend!" Amal announced.

Nafees tried to look nonchalant, blowing on her fingernails and buffing them on her shirt.

"Really? A new boyfriend?" I couldn't believe it. "Another one? Already?"

"Whoa…one question at a time, but the answers are yes, yes, and yes."

"Tell, tell!" Heba was practically shouting.

Nafees beamed. "It was kismet. I didn't want to go with my dad to the post office but he made me and… Bingo! Damien's so cute, one hundred times cuter than Marcus! We exchanged phone numbers and my father was so busy with the oversized box he was shipping to Pakistan, he didn't even have a clue!"

"I bet he thought you were cute too, huh?" I asked. "Did you kiss yet? Did you?"

"Of course we kissed," she said.

"In the post office?"

"Don't be silly!" Nafees snorted. "Much, *much* later!"

Amal, Sehr, Heba, and I looked at each other. Nafees had done it again. How did she manage it?

Zayd burst into the room. "I've been looking everywhere for you!" he panted. "You better come fast, Aliya! Mom's really mad at you!"

"We'll talk next Sunday," I promised Nafees. "I've got to go now."

"Not a word to anyone, Aliya!" Nafees called after me. "Not to your parents, not to anyone."

"I won't tell," I reassured her. "I promise."

I turned to Zayd and gave him a shove. "It's Aliya Apa, dork!"

On the way home from Eid prayers, sandwiched between OCD and Zayd, I thought about poor Sehr.

"What's the matter?" Baba asked, looking at me in the rearview mirror.

"Nothing," I said.

"Why you suddenly so *chup chaap*, hanh?" OCD asked, wiggling and crushing me some more. "Why you so quiet?"

I told everyone about what had happened to Sehr and her decision to remove her hijab.

"I don't blame her," Mom said. "These days it just seems to provoke people."

"Some people. Not all," Baba reminded her.

"Some is more than none. We were doing just fine until 9/11."

I didn't know which way to feel anymore. At first, Marwa's hijab had seemed like a red flag in the face of a bull—an invitation to anger and resentment. But now, I was beginning to wonder. More and more, Marwa reminded me of a ship that stayed true to its course, no matter how strong the winds or hard the rains. I reminded myself to write Allah about this in my next letter.

OCD was doing her best to follow the conversation, but we talked way too fast for her. *"Vhaat? Vhaat* they saying?" she asked.

"Nothing," I replied.

Obviously upset about being left out, OCD crossed her hands over her chest. "Nobody vhants to talk to us," she pouted.

I felt sorry for her. "I will," I offered. "What do you want to talk about?"

OCD sniffed and squirmed. She turned her body away from me and stared out the window.

Her prayer beads brushed against my arm. "We can talk about these," I said, trying to placate her. "They're so beautiful. May I hold them, Choti Dahdi?"

OCD turned to me. "Aii, why?"

"I'll be really careful. I promise."

She snorted but I could tell that she was feeling better.

"Hold lightly, lightly," she commanded, handing the beads over reluctantly.

"I'll be really gentle," I assured her, but before I could get a decent look at them OCD thrust her hand out.

"Time up!" She snatched the beads back from me. "When you marry, we put them in nice box with red ribbon to give to you as wedding gift." She nudged Mom's shoulder. "Did you hear what we told your daughter? We said we vhill give our beautiful beads to her on wedding day!"

"Thanks," I said. But would it have killed her to let me hold them a little longer?

I didn't talk to my parents about Nafees, but I couldn't stop thinking about her. She'd kissed Marcus *and* Damien. As Amma might say, she was the honey—shimmering, gleaming and luscious—that brought the foolish fly; she was the biscuit that brought the frisky puppy. *I* wanted to be the biscuit. *I* wanted to be the honey.

What did a kiss on the lips feel like? I put the back of my hand to my lips. I closed my eyes and imagined Josh kissing me. I got goose pimply. Was that how it felt? Suddenly, it didn't matter that Nafees couldn't go dancing in a club. It didn't matter that she couldn't buy music or wear shorts. I'd probably trade those things in for a boyfriend and a kiss on the lips in a second!

"How's your Steps to Success assignment coming along?" Baba asked, disturbing my daydream.

"Okay," I mumbled. "It's not due until April."

"I hope it's turning into more than just one long gripe session," Mom said.

"Mo-om!" I cried. "That's so mean!"

"I'm just trying to be helpful, Aliya. I wish you'd take input with better grace."

"Exactly, Aliya," added Zayd.

"She's Aliya Apa to you, mister!" Mom and Baba said in one big voice together.

My grandmothers were waiting for our return with big smiles on their faces and hugs at the ready.

"Where's our *Eidi*?" Zayd asked, too eager for gift time—his favorite part of the holiday—to be polite.

Amma and Badi Amma put golden envelopes in our hands. We ripped them open and found crisp dollar bills—twenty-one for each of us—for our college fund.

OCD went straight up to my room; she hobbled back down the stairs a little while later. "Come here," she called. "Juldi, juldi!"

"Yes, Choti Dahdi, what do you want?" I sighed, bracing myself to run another errand for her. Lately she'd been wearing Zayd and me down with shouted commands: *Bring this from* my *room! Take that to* my *room! Put this in* my *room!*

But OCD grinned broadly. "I don't vhaant," she said. "I geeve." She thrust our Eidi in our hands—seven folded dollar bills. She cupped my chin in her hand, brought her fingers to her lips, and kissed them with a big *um-mah*! Then she did the same to Zayd.

I felt guilty for thinking bad thoughts about her, so I ran to the kitchen to bring her a glass of water. "Here is some *vhaater* for you, Choti Dahdi."

Then it was time to open the pile of presents from our parents. I didn't get designer jeans or an iPod or anything like that, but I did get a new cell phone, some jewelry, and a gift card to my favorite store. My very own cell phone! I couldn't wait to show Winnie.

Amma had everything under control for our Eid party. The plates and forks were lined up, the food had been spooned into large dishes, and the *sheer khorma* shimmied in a large bowl. Zayd and I asked for a little taste, but Mom shook her head. "It's the only dessert," she said. "I don't want it eaten up before the party starts."

The guests arrived in spurts and I ran back and forth carrying all the coats and scarves upstairs. Each time someone came to the door, exuberant cries of "Eid Mubarak!" rang out. Everyone was thankful for a successful month of fasting. We had been good Muslims and upstanding citizens; we had curbed anger and temptation, read from the holy Quran, and given help to the poor by sending money to India. Now we were ready to celebrate!

I stuck close by Amma's side, helping with the food first and then with the heavily spiced milky teas we served after dinner. When it was time for dessert, I offered to take the sheer khorma to the table.

"Don't trip," Amma cautioned. "Go very, very slowly, one step at a time."

"Geez, Amma," I said. "I'm doing fine. Stop worrying so much."

At that precise moment, Zayd charged up and bumped my elbow. "Watch out!" I cried. The sheer khorma sloshed about in the bowl.

"Careful," Amma called. "Don't spill, don't spill!"

"I'm not going to!" I shuffled forward, one cautious step at a time. "Why does everyone make such a big deal about things around here! Sheesh!" I made my way to the destination and set the bowl down carefully.

Zayd crept up to the bowl and peered in. "Uh-oh!" He scrunched up his nose. "There's a bug in the sheer khorma!"

"What? Are you sure?"

"Yup," he insisted. "I can see it."

"It's a raisin, you idiot!"

"No way! Raisins don't have wings."

I looked again. What if my brother was right?

Amma came running, armed with a wooden spoon. "Where is this bug?" she hissed.

"There it is…see?"

"It's not a bug, mad boy!" Amma said. "It's a raisin."

"It does look like a bug," I said.

"Raisin or bug, I am going to scoop it out," Amma announced.

"Ewww," I said.

"Ewww, nothing," snapped Amma. "This is a lot of sheer khorma and it's our only dessert." She dipped the spoon into the bowl and lifted the bug out.

Choti Dahdi hurried in. "Aii, vhaat happened?"

"Nothing, Aunt," Amma said. "It's just that the children think this is a bug."

"Show me, show me!" Choti Dahdi put her nose an inch away from the spoon.

"What do you think?" Amma asked.

"Go, go! This is no bug. It's a fat raisin!" She lifted the bug/raisin off the spoon and popped it in her mouth. "Silly, silly children!"

"Ewww!" Zayd and I cried at the same time.

OCD smacked her lips in delight. "All is vhell," she declared. "All is vhell."

Zayd's such an idiot!

December 10
11:00 p.m.

Dear Allah,

Mom says it's late but I'm not sleepy. So much happened on this special day. Some of it was really great but some wasn't. I'll tell You the bad part first. It's Sehr. Just a few days ago it was her sister, and now it's her! I can't believe it. Why, though? It's just a piece of cloth… and they were minding their own business anyway, right? She acts brave but I think she's scared. And then I think about Marwa (Amal too) and I get really confused. Why did You make some of us braver than others? Marwa told me once I should just try to be me, but when I am scared, I want to be like her.

It was a great Eid and I got great presents.

Yours truly,

A.

PS Eid Mubarak! Or Eid Mubrook, as Marwa would say.

Campaign Highs

The Glen Meadow student council campaign was firmly underway. With only a few more days left to get out the vote, everyone scurried about, trying to get things done.

Josh didn't seem worried. He sauntered down the hallway, cool as a cucumber, shaking hands and giving thumbs-up as though the election was already neatly wrapped up and tucked away in his hip pocket.

Winnie and I put up my posters. Madison, Leah, and Carly followed behind making sure the spacing was even. We had worked very hard on the slogans.

VOTE FOR ALIYA! SHE WILL GO TO BAT FOR YOU.
(for the jocks)

VOTE FOR ALIYA! SHE CARES. SHE WILL WATCH YOUR BACK.
(for the unpopular kids and the nerds)

VOTE FOR ALIYA! SHE IS TRUE TO HER WORD.
(for the rest of the kids)

Juliana strutted like a peacock. Her life-sized posters showed her in a perfect X-shaped cheerleader leap, hair flying and pompoms shaking.

REACH FOR NEW HEIGHTS! VOTE FOR JULIANA!

Marwa kept to herself. Sometimes I saw her in quiet conversations with kids, but she wasn't making a lot of noise like the rest of us. Her posters weren't that great either. I guess she didn't have a campaign manager like Winnie giving her good advice. But mostly I suspected her hijab was getting in the way.

When Juliana started handing out friendship bracelets and baseball cards, I got really worried. An alarming number of kids were sporting the bracelets now and the boys were already trading cards.

"Is she allowed to do that?" I asked Winnie.

"I don't think there are any rules against it," Winnie said. "But this makes me nervous. You should bring something in as quickly as possible."

"Mom could bake a batch of cupcakes," I said.

"Tell her to make samosas. I love her samosas!"

"I don't know… Kids might not like them…"

"You worry too much."

"It won't work anyway," I said. "We're not even allowed to bring food to share anymore."

"Oh yeah!" Winnie growled. "I forgot. That rule sucks big time!"

"We need to do *something*, though," I said. "Juliana's killing us with all her handouts."

"Let's check our to-do list." Winnie ran through each item. "'Put up posters.' We've done that. 'Talk up the campaign during lunch.' Check. Here's one we haven't tried yet. 'Get proactive!' Talk to Josh. He definitely holds the ticket to the boys' block."

My hands suddenly got clammy.

"Hold on!"

I couldn't talk to Josh. How could I? I got tongue-tied when he even looked at me.

"You talk to him, Winnie. Please, please, please?"

The next morning Juliana stopped me in the hall. "You're the one who did it!" she hissed.

I had no idea what she was talking about.

"Don't act all innocent!" she screamed. "You pulled my best poster down! It was there by the front door yesterday and then today, poof, it's gone!"

"I didn't do it!" I protested. I *wouldn't*. I'd be grounded for life if I ever did anything that backhanded and sneaky.

By ten o'clock, there was more bad news. Two of my posters were missing too.

"I bet Juliana's getting back at you," Winnie suggested.

"What should I do?"

"You should go to Mrs. Doyle, pronto!" Leah said.

"I can't," I said. "I don't know for sure if it was Juliana. It could have been Austin. He's the one who really hates me."

We checked out Marwa's posters, but they were all still there.

"I don't know what she was thinking when she made these posters," I said to Leah. "There's not one thing in them about her."

Kids are the future.

Kids don't need talking to. They need listening to.

Kids find everything in nothing.
Grown-ups find nothing in everything.

"Hi!" Marwa said. "What do you think of my posters?"

I hadn't even noticed her standing nearby.

"Um…you can't even see your name," I pointed out. "And they're all pretty small."

"I think they're kind of neat," Leah said.

Madison nodded.

I turned to them in surprise. "Really?"

"Yup. It's like they're talking to me personally," Madison said.

"They make kids feel important, you know?" Leah added.

"Thanks!" Marwa said. "Speaking of posters, I heard some disappeared today."

"I bet it's Austin," I said. "He never liked me all that much, but now he really hates me."

"Yeah, but he doesn't hate Juliana," Winnie said. "And her posters disappeared too. But Marwa's are still up. Hmm…totally confusing!"

"I have a theory about the posters," Marwa said. "I'm thinking that it might be the tape."

"You mean the posters are falling off the wall?" I asked. "Yours seem to be fine."

"Precisely." Marwa smiled. "They're much smaller than the others."

"They need to be much *bigger*," I said. "And more colorful too."

"Her posters are teeny, but the message isn't," Winnie said.

"It's not the tape," I insisted. "It's either Juliana or Austin or both of them."

"I really, *really* like Marwa's message," Madison said.

"Yeah, me too," added Leah.

Juliana's friendship bracelets were a huge hit. I had to get proactive really fast!

Reluctantly, I went to look for Josh. I found him on the basketball court, in the middle of a game. He made three baskets in a row—*bam…bam…bam*—with no effort at all. I stood on the sideline, trying to decide what I was going to say and how I was going to say it. Before I knew it, the recess bell rang. Josh threw the ball to Matt and walked off the court.

I took an extra big breath. "Er…hi."

Josh looked at me blankly. "Hi."

"Great game," I said.

"Thanks."

"I'm going to vote for you."

"Cool."

When I didn't say anything more, he started to walk away.

"I'm running for class rep in Mrs. Doyle's room." My words came out in a breathless rush as I hurried to catch up with him.

"Cool," he said again, without breaking a step.

I watched him go. *Stupid, stupid, stupid!* I said to myself.

But then he stopped and turned around, squinting at me.

Maybe he wanted to ask me to help him with his campaign or something like that. I sucked in my breath and waited for him to speak.

"What's your name again?" he called.

"A…Aliya."

"Right!" He strode away without a look back at me.

He hadn't even known my name.

More posters were missing the following week.

Mr. Belotti walked by, carrying a tall stack of brown paper towel packages.

"Good morning, Mr. Belotti," I said. "I was wondering…have you seen…do you know anything about my posters? We had stuck them up in the halls and they, um… seem to be missing."

"Oh, they were yours, were they?" He glowered at me. "You kids should know better than to use such cheap tape."

"Huh?"

"You need stronger tape for the posters, kiddo. They fell down and made a mess of the hallway. I had to throw some of them out."

"Did you have to get rid of them?" I protested. "We worked very hard to make them."

"Not my job to pick up after you, kiddo," Mr. Belotti growled.

Marwa was right! It was the tape. Amma's old roll of tape from the basement wasn't strong enough to hold my posters up. But defective tape didn't explain Juliana's missing poster.

"Maybe her designer tape was old too!" Winnie said when I told her what Mr. Belotti had said.

"I guess her posters were so big that no tape could hold them up," I said.

"Yeah," Winnie chuckled. "As big as her head."

Wednesday, December 11
9:30 p.m.

Dear Allah,

I suppose it wouldn't be the end of the world if I lost. I feel pretty good about being in the race in the first place. In a way it's like Ramadan: a challenge to be met. Badi Amma is very proud of me. She can't stop talking about the campaign. When OCD heard us discussing it, she asked, "Aii, what is estoodent kunsul?"

I may not win this race, but I've come up with a few things to try anyway:

Figure out a way to get attention away from Juliana.

Talk to Josh again; convince him this time; speak up!

Compliment Ellen on her new haircut.

Help Tracy with her social studies homework.

Write my speech.

Talk to Amma about the butterflies in my stomach.

Yours truly,

A

PS I can get stronger tape for my posters, but I wish they had a stronger message (like Marwa's).

OCD's Diamonds

OCD sprawled comfortably on the recliner in the TV room, fingering her prayer beads and reciting Allahu Akbar, Allahu Akbar with her eyes closed. Her beads clicked rhythmically—each one the size of a pea but as clear and luminous as a sparkling water drop. If someone didn't know any better, they'd think my OCD was a very rich old lady.

"Where did you get your beads?" I asked.

"*Makah Sharif,*" OCD replied. "Holy Mecca. Al humdu lillah, very, very expensive!"

"On your pilgrimage?" I asked.

"Yes, yes. Ninety-nine beads. A bead for each one of Allah's great attributes. Come, come. Recite them for us. Now! Juldi, juldi!"

I shook my head, ashamed. I couldn't.

"Aii!" she said. "Tch…tch."

"The beads are beautiful, Choti Dahdi," I said.

OCD nodded and continued reciting Allah's praise.

"You should say 'thank you' when someone pays you a compliment," I muttered.

"Eh? Kya bole? Vhaat you say?"

"Nothing," I mumbled.

"Then why were lips moving up and down going pitter, pitter?"

I snapped my book shut and turned on the TV. An advertisement for a new program came on.

"*La hol walla!*" OCD screeched. "The ujjad woman is showing legs up to *there!*"

She stormed out, not noticing that her prayer beads had fallen from the pocket of her abbayah. I opened my mouth to speak but quickly changed my mind. Not yet. First I'd make her sweat a little to make her pay for the zillion errands she made me run and for the shrieking and criticizing too.

The beads caught the light and glittered like stars. Winnie'd think they were gorgeous too. I'd show them to her and return them before OCD even noticed them missing. I tucked the prayer beads away in my pocket.

The next day, my friends gawked at the beads I had twisted around my wrist. Pleased at their reaction, I told them that it was a diamond bracelet that had been in my family for a long time.

It wasn't long before Juliana heard about them. When we were lining up for lunch, she leaned over and said to me, "I heard you have some sort of bracelet."

"I do." My face felt hot.

"Let me see."

I held out my wrist.

"Those are diamonds?" she asked. When I nodded, she raised an eyebrow. "No way!"

"Way!" I said.

"Yeah, right!" she muttered.

Juliana obviously didn't want me to know it, but I could tell she was impressed. She told some other girls and they told their friends and I soon was the center of attention.

"She's jealous," I told Winnie gleefully. "She's bright green with envy!"

Winnie gave me a high five. "Are you kidding?" she exclaimed. "Who wouldn't be?"

Fifteen minutes before the end of the last class, I raised my hand to ask permission to go to the bathroom. The jingle of the beads drew everyone's eyes again, making me feel like a Hollywood celebrity.

I danced down the hall, swerved toward the girls' room, and grabbed the door handle. As I went through the door, the bracelet snagged on the latch. *Ping, ping, ping*…a shower of beads bounced onto the bathroom floor and scattered everywhere!

I gaped stupidly for a second or two, then dropped to my knees. With shaking hands, I chased down eleven errant attributes of Allah. My heart hammered in my chest and a buzz droned in my ear. In a flash, my celebrity glow vanished and I was left with the very scary prospect of my great-grandaunt's wrath. My hands shook as I collected the rest of the beads and stuffed them into my pocket.

"What's wrong with you?" Winnie asked me as we settled into our seats on the bus.

"I don't feel so good," I admitted.

"Are you going to be sick? It's a good thing we're almost home!"

Home was the last place I wanted to be. OCD was there, her broken beads were in my pocket, and I had absolutely no idea what I was going to tell her.

OCD pounced like a hungry tigress as soon as I stepped through the door. "Have you seen them?" she demanded.

My heart hammered in my chest. "Assalam alaikum, Choti Dahdi," I said, trying to buy some time.

"Yes, yes… Assalam alaikum," she replied. "Have you seen our prayer beads?"

"Prayer beads?" I tried to sound casual but my insides were shaking like leaves in a hurricane.

"Aii! What prayer beads, she asks!" She turned to Amma in disgust.

"Choti Dahdi can't find her prayer beads," Amma said. "I was hoping you knew where they were."

"I don't know anything," I muttered, squirming a little.

"I don't either," Zayd added.

Amma looked slightly defeated. "We'll find them, Aunt dear. They didn't walk away and certainly no one took them."

"*Ai hai! Ai hai!*" OCD lamented. "We will ask Bibi Sayeda for help."

Bibi Sayeda was a saintly person who helped people find lost things. Once you had found your lost object, you were required to do a form of obeisance by making fourteen salaams to her, followed by giving alms to the poor. The amazing thing was that Bibi Sayeda had died a very long time ago, but according to Choti Dahdi she could still help from the other side.

"Yes, you do that," Amma encouraged.

I escaped to the sanctuary of Zayd's room, but after a few minutes Amma walked in. "I came to look here one more time—" She stopped midsentence and raised an eyebrow. "What's wrong, Aliya? You don't look so well."

The concern on my grandmother's face was more than I could take. I burst out crying and my whole body began to tremble.

Amma quickly wrapped me up in her arms. "What's wrong, Meri Jaan?" she asked, rocking me gently back and forth. "Are you all right?"

"N-no," I sobbed. "I...I am n-not all right. Nothing is all r-right!"

I told my grandmother the whole story—about Juliana's posters and the bracelets and the eye rolling and then I told her about Choti Dahdi's prayer beads and the bathroom door latch.

I waited for my grandmother to say something, but for the longest time she didn't speak a word.

"Amma?" I cried, looking into her eyes.

"Meri Jaan," she finally sighed. "You chose the wrong way to impress your friends. Diamonds don't matter. Truth and honesty do. That is what people remember us for, in the end."

"I was going to return them. Honest," I wept. "I didn't know everything would go this wrong."

"A wrong can be made right," Amma said. She held me and let me cry and cry. When I had calmed down, she said, "I think you know what you must do."

"Do I have to?" I pleaded. "Couldn't we tell her the prayer beads were under the cushions or something?"

"We could, but *should* we?"

"I guess not," I admitted.

"We must own up to our mistakes. I'm afraid that takes courage but it is the right thing to do. Do you have the courage, Meri Jaan?"

No, I wanted to admit to her, *I don't*. I was a famous Fraidy Cat. I was scared of Austin, threatened by Marwa, awed by Juliana, and nervous around Josh, and all I wanted to do was run and hide from Choti Dahdi.

"Meri Jaan?" my grandmother prodded, but I shook my head forcefully. She sighed.

"Listen to this true story." She hugged me closer. "A little girl planted a mango seed in dry earth. The well was a great distance away and the road was rocky and sun was blazing and the bucket was heavy but the little girl was a brave soldier. She walked and walked until she had blisters on her feet, but she kept going because she had to fetch water for her seed. When the mango ripened, the girl took a bite. And straightaway, she forgot about the blisters but she remembered the sweet, sweet taste of the mango for a very long time."

It was Badi Amma's story. I had heard the story of the garden of my *imaan* a million times. Amma had added the part about the blisters but the rest of the story was the same. I closed my eyes, snuggled closer, and willed myself to think about the mango seed. I went deeper this time. Then I pushed away from my grandmother's soft bosom and met her hard gaze.

"Yes, Amma," I said slowly. "I think I can be brave."

"Shabaash! Well done!" My grandmother drew me back to her. "You can stop worrying now. You're looking at the world's best fixer-upper, young lady, or did you forget? My job is easy. Yours is so much harder in comparison and I am oh so proud that you are ready to tackle it!"

With each step forward, I wished I could take ten in the opposite direction, but I kept going. "Be brave," my inner voice urged. "Be brave."

I heard OCD muttering to Bibi Sayeda, promising those fourteen salaams if only she could find her beads. I watched as she looked behind the drapes and peeked in the fireplace.

She opened and closed cupboards and pantry doors; she pulled cans of soup and vegetables from the shelves. She even peeked into the garbage pail, with a thumb and finger pinching her nostrils. She was clearly desperate.

"Choti Dahdi," I called out softly. I don't think she heard because she continued her frantic search. "Choti Dahdi," I tried again, a little bit louder this time. "I have something to tell you…"

I told her everything and it wasn't so bad after all. Choti Dahdi lectured me about the evils of stealing and I didn't argue. She said it made Allah unhappy and I nodded in shame. But she also added that Allah is always pleased with people who ask for His forgiveness. I promised I'd ask. "Cross my heart," I added.

"Aii!" snorted Choti Dahdi. "What is this 'Cross my heart'?"

Important Victories

Madison came running up to us in the hall. "Hey, Aliya," she panted. "Juliana's saying horrible things about you!"

"What's the witch saying now?" Winnie asked before I could react.

"She's going around telling people you're toast!"

"I'm what? What exactly does she mean by that?" I cried.

"Toast. That means you're finished! It's over for you."

"I know what it means!" I said. "Why is she saying it?"

"Dirty politics," Winnie speculated. "That's what this is. She's shifting her strategy from buying votes to negative campaigning."

"What should I do?" I asked.

"We should start our own smear campaign," Winnie said. "We can spread the word that a vote for Juliana will contribute to the ruination of the school."

"I don't know," I said. "I don't think my Mom or Amma will allow that. They'd want me to be truthful and honest."

Juliana, Nicole, and Morgan stood behind me in the lunch line.

"*Maar...vaa.* What kind of name is that anyway?" Juliana giggled. "*Maar...vaa!*"

"And get a load of the scarf she has on today," Nicole said.

Juliana snorted. "Does she think she's making some sort of a fashion statement?"

"And how about that gross stuff she's always eating?" Morgan added.

My ears were hot and my heart was pounding. Without thinking, I whirled around. "You're worse than Austin! Her name is Marwa!"

"What?"

"Marwa doesn't wear her hijab for fashion. She does it because she thinks it's the right thing for a Muslim girl to do."

I think that startled Juliana. "Whatever," she muttered.

"And it's mean to talk behind someone's back," I added.

Juliana, Nicole, and Morgan stared at me. Winnie's jaw had dropped; she looked back and forth between me and Juliana.

"How would you know?" Juliana asked. "Are you a Mos...lem, or whatever it's called?"

"*Mus*-lim." I emphasized the proper *U* vowel sound in the first syllable. "You know very well I am."

"So why don't you wear a funny scarf too?"

I started to explain about personal decisions and interpretations—things that Mom was always telling me about—but I changed my mind. Instead, I just said, "It's hurtful and cowardly to talk behind someone's back. If you have something to say, bad or good, you should be brave enough to say it to her face."

Juliana, Morgan, and Nicole just stood there silently. That made me feel good.

"Marwa's really nice," I said. "You should try to get to know her."

"Who says we are remotely interested in knowing her?" Juliana had found her bearing again.

"If you aren't," I said, "you're really missing out. She can be a very good friend." I started to leave. Then I turned back. "And by the way, that gross stuff? It's just feta cheese. The Greeks eat it too."

"Can you believe it?" Juliana sneered. "The cat just let go of someone's tongue!"

"Way to go, Aliya!" Winnie thumped my back so hard that she almost knocked me over. "I can't believe you did that!"

I had just stood up to Juliana! And I had done it without help! Still, my heart was thumping in my chest and my mouth was dry. I knew that they were probably rolling their eyes and smirking. But maybe their laughter was now tinged with embarrassment.

After lunch, we found Madison and Leah outside huddled against the wall, stomping their legs and trying to keep warm.

"What was going on in the line back there?" Madison asked. "It looked like you were really telling Juliana off!"

"She was being a big jerk," I said.

"You should have seen Aliya," Winnie told them. "I've never seen her like that. I was so proud of her!"

"Thanks, Winnie," I said.

We hopped on one foot and the other and did jumping jacks just to keep the blood circulating. I didn't notice Austin had walked up until I heard him behind me.

"Watch out! The Alien's leaping!" he yelled. "And if you aren't careful, the Alien will bulldoze you over!"

"What's wrong with him?" Madison asked.

"What's *wrong* with him is there's nothing *right* about him," I said.

"Get lost, creep!" Leah shouted.

Suddenly I thought of someone else I wanted to see before we had to go back inside.

"Hey, where are you going?" Winnie called out. "Austin's not going to bother you now; he's going away!"

I walked over to the picnic bench. But no one was there.

Thursday, December 12
7:30 p.m.

Dear Allah,
    I told Juliana off today. Yesss!
    But I couldn't find Marwa.
                    Yours truly,
                    A

PS I have so much to tell her!

Two Toads

The Glen Meadow Student Council school elections were two days away and excitement was building by the hour. Voting for the executive council was in the gymnasium but class representatives—one from each homeroom—were being elected in their own homerooms.

The campaign was at a fever pitch. Marwa was the only one who still seemed cool and collected. The rest of us zipped around her in high gear, like wind-up toys just let loose.

My father told me that a campaign speech was terribly important, especially if one wanted to sway the undecided block. "You sound a bit tentative," he said, reviewing what I had written. "You need to sound sure about yourself. Your words should exude confidence. You need to convey that you are up to the job. Don't be afraid to embellish your strengths." Sentence by sentence, he underlined phrases, struck through words, scribbled a few notes, and drew smiley faces beside the parts he liked.

I put my old speech on the table and next to it, a brand new piece of paper. First, I jotted down all my strengths:

Kindhearted
Responsible
Conscientious
Hardworking
Trustworthy
Good friend
Persistent — in other words, does not give up

And then I started over on my speech.

When I was finally done, I practiced several times in front of Mom and Amma and Badi Amma. OCD was helpful in her own crazy sort of way. First she instructed me to stand tall. When my posture didn't satisfy her, she tried to show me how, even though she still looked crooked to me. Then she told me to speak more clearly and not eat up my words.

"How do you know I am mumbling?" I asked. "You don't even speak English that well."

"Aii!" she screeched. "We know English. Hello, bye, come, go, God Bless *Umrica*... You see?"

"She is absolutely right," Mom said. "Please enunciate better and pull yourself out of your slouch, will you?"

Our music teacher had given us some lines to say to practice our enunciation in class. I repeated them at home until my throat was dry and my voice hoarse: *Two toads terribly tired trotting down the road. Two toads terribly tired trotting down the road... Two toads terribly tired... Two toads...*

Winnie gave me last-minute instructions in homeroom.
"Take deep breaths," she said. "Close your eyes and count
backwards from ten…slowly."

My hands were clammy and my throat felt dry. I decided
to go over the speech in my head one last time. When I
couldn't remember my opening line, I panicked! Frantically
I dug in my pocket for the scrap of paper and reviewed
everything word by word.

*Hello, friends. I am Aliya and I want to represent you
in the school council. I am the right person for the job. Let
me tell you why. I am a hard worker and a pretty good
student. I am a good friend and you can depend on me
and trust me because I am very responsible and I will
never let you down. I will do a better job than my worthy
opponent because I am conscientious and caring. I will
listen carefully and I will sit down with you. We can
talk about your problems or you can write down your
concerns and put them in a suggestion box and I promise
to read everything. Believe me, no problem will be too
small or unimportant.*

*We have a great school but we can improve it. Here
are some ideas to make us a more caring school: We
should do more to help the poor and the victims of
hurricanes. I think we waste a lot of food, don't you?
We should stop doing that. We should give leftovers to the*

*poor people. We should be more conservation minded and
we should stop wasting so much paper.*

*I have fun ideas too. We could have a flea market for
kids someday or maybe even help kids set up a business or
have a talent show, because everyone is special in some
way. I have many more ideas and I promise I will listen to
yours. Please vote for me. Thank you.*

When it was time for the speeches, Juliana sprang out of
her seat and strode up like a warrior to the front of the room.
She swept her hands over her perfect hair and smoothed
down the sides of her perfect new sweater. "Hello, everyone," she said cheerily. "You all know who I am so I don't
have to introduce myself. But I will tell you that I want to be
your class rep and I want your vote."

She went on to tell us why she was the better choice and
gave reasons why a vote for her was a vote for success and
reform. But I wasn't listening anymore; I was too busy chew-
ing on my nails and going over my speech in my head.

When Juliana was done, everyone clapped loudly and
she bowed with a dramatic flourish. The applause felt end-
less. I looked at Winnie nervously and she gave me a hearty
thumbs-up. Mrs. Holmes turned to me. I looked over at Winnie again and she smiled and crossed her fingers. "Good
luck," she mouthed silently.

I walked to the front of the room, aware that everyone's
attention was focused on me. I pulled myself out of my
slouch and scanned my audience. Twenty-six pairs of eyes

were focused on me. Twenty-six pairs of ears were tuned in on me. I opened my mouth to speak and this is what popped out: *"Two toads terribly tired trotting down the road."*

At first the silence was deafening, but then the room exploded. Juliana rolled her eyes and Morgan and Nicole doubled up. Winnie dropped her head into her hands and Leah and Madison avoided my eyes. I was mortified.

I laughed nervously. "Ooops… I'm sorry. I got mixed up. You know how Mrs. Benson had us repeat…you know, in music? Okay, anyway… I'm going to start over again."

I looked to Mrs. Doyle for help; she nodded sympathetically and motioned me on. I took a deep breath, just as Winnie had advised.

Hello, friends, I began, flawlessly this time. *I am Aliya and I want to represent you in the school council.*

When I was done, I walked back to my seat quickly and sat down. I felt a little numb and my mouth was so dry I could barely swallow. I did hear some applause; some kids clapped more heartily than others. Winnie's claps, I noticed, were the loudest. Juliana's were the phoniest.

"How did I do?" I whispered to Winnie.

She held up her thumb. "Great speech."

"Thanks," I mumbled.

"Except maybe what happened at the beginning?"

"Let's not talk about that, okay?" I said.

Voting began at twelve o'clock. Five minutes later, it was completed.

"I think you clinched it," Winnie said.

Mrs. Doyle rapped for attention. I sucked in air and crossed my fingers under my desk. Juliana, Morgan, and Nicole locked arms and hung on to each other like links in a chain.

Mrs. Doyle began with a motivational speech: *Regardless of the outcome, I congratulate those with the courage to participate in this democratic process,* et cetera, et cetera.

Juliana's finger twirled and her mouth moved, mimicking our teacher.

At last Mrs. Doyle turned to the whiteboard to report the outcome of the election. In her elegant cursive, she wrote *A-l-i-y-a*, then *J-u-l-i-a-n-a*. She put a great big 1 next to my name and a great big 1 next to Juliana's. We were neck and neck so far!

Then Mrs. Doyle slanted a great big 0 next to the 1 by my name. Next to Juliana's she wrote a great, big…6!

Aliya: 10

Juliana: 16

It was all over. The class had spoken. Winnie squeezed my hand. "I'm sorry," she whispered. She brought her finger and thumb together so they almost touched. "It was this close. You would've definitely been the best representative."

I appreciated her encouraging words, but I felt like the rug had been yanked from under me. Friendship bracelets and baseball cards had trumped ninety-nine fake diamonds.

I scrambled to remember Badi Amma's emergency pep talk. It was something about being proud of myself no matter what, but my great-grandmother's words didn't provide much comfort now. Juliana was the class rep. I was not. I was simply Aliya. Aliya, the loser.

Aliya, the weirdo.

Aliya, the alien.

Aliya, the girl who didn't have a boyfriend.

I was still reeling from my defeat when Winnie slid back into her desk. She had heard some news on the way back from the girls' room.

"You're not going to believe this," she gasped. "Not in a million, trillion years!"

For a split second, I had a wild thought. Had Mrs. Doyle miscounted the votes? My heart raced. "What?" I hissed. "What happened?"

There'd been an upset in Mr. Gallagher's homeroom. Marwa had won!

I couldn't believe my ears! Marwa had beat Camden to become the fifth-grade student representative to the council from Mr. Gallagher's homeroom! I was completely flummoxed! How could it be? How had she done it?

"What's her secret, Winnie?"

"It's no secret," she said. "Marwa's a pretty gutsy kid."

"I guess you're right," I said. "There was always something special about her. I knew it from day one. I just couldn't figure out what until now."

This was huge. Marwa, newly arrived from Morocco by way of Michigan. Marwa, the Muslim girl in hijab with smelly cheese in her lunch box, had made a statement at Glen Meadow School! She was a winner!

I was happy for her and I wanted her to know it. After class, I elbowed my way through a human wall three kids deep.

"Nice job, Marwa," I said. "You did it! You'll make a great class rep."

"Insha' Allah," she said. "God willing. And you?"

I pointed my thumb downward and shook my head.

"I'm so sorry," she said. "I had my fingers crossed for you."

"You should've heard Marwa's speech," Maggie gushed. "It was totally inspiring."

That made me wonder. Did Marwa win because her speech had been more forceful than mine? Did she have better word choice?

"What did you say exactly?" I asked Marwa.

Sarah answered for her. "She stood there, looking so calm and serene. And then, she said—and I quote—'Friends, we are in this together. We can make a difference if we stick to each other like glue. This is not about you or about me…it is about us, working together and working hand in hand!'"

Marwa smiled. "Those weren't my exact words," she said.

"Oh well, maybe not a direct quote, but close enough," Sarah said.

I didn't get it. Wasn't that my message too? Didn't I also say something along those lines?

Maybe the difference wasn't in the message but in the messenger?

Losers and Winners

"Did you congratulate Juliana?" Baba asked.

I hadn't. Her smile had looked mean and gloating, so I'd avoided her for the rest of the day.

"I hate her, Baba!" I cried.

"That's a pretty strong word," my father said.

"I mean it! She always beats me at everything and she rolls her eyes when I walk by and she's always telling me how much she hates spicy foods!"

"Hmm," Baba said. "But what if you had walked up to her right away and congratulated her on her victory? It might have made a lasting impact."

I stared at him. Had he not heard a single word I said? "She's got so much going for her: great outfits and fabulous vacations and a really fancy car, and what do I have, huh?"

Baba ruffled my hair. "You've got plenty too, honey."

"Yeah, right!" I sniffled.

My father drew me close. "You have a loving family and a nice home. You have a great life too."

I hugged my dad back. I did have a great life; it was just that Juliana also had Josh on top of everything else. "Anyway, plenty of people congratulated her," I muttered. "She didn't need to hear it from me."

"But she did. An Aliya handshake—why that would have been something else!" Baba smiled. "It doesn't hurt to be nice, you know."

"Tell that to her!" I said. "She's the mean one!"

"That would be her parents' job," my father said.

"Fat chance," I said. "Her dad doesn't even live with her and I bet her mom doesn't tell her either because she's probably mean too!"

"A twist of *good*, a sprinkle of *kind*, and a dash of *nice*," Baba said in a dopey voice.

"Huh?"

Baba smiled. "It's a recipe for getting along."

"You say the weirdest things, Baba," I said. "Stop right now!"

Tuesday, December 17
9:00 p.m.

Dear Allah,

The big boulder that was crushing my heart has lifted a little. I have practiced some lines to say to Juliana. "Nice job!" "Congrats!" "Way to go!" I know Baba is right about being nice, but being nice to Juliana?

This is my plan: I will shake her hand and I will tell her that she'll probably make a pretty good class rep. And if she rolls her eyes at me, I will say, "You're quite welcome, I'm sure," in a sarcastic voice and walk away and never try to be nice to her again. I mean it!

Marwa won! At first it was hard to believe, but I'm not surprised anymore.

It was never her hijab, was it?

Yours truly,

A

PS It's not what's on your head that matters—it's what's inside it. I know I said this before, but I like the sound of the words. Don't you?

Juliana walked by, popping her gum and accompanied by her entourage.

"Congrats, Juliana," I said.

Part of me felt like a phony but another part of me was remembering something I'd heard recently. *What's wrong with making someone feel good? It's only a teeny white lie and it's not hurting anyone.* I could almost hear Marwa speaking in my ear.

Juliana blew a big bubble and I waited for the sharp pop. But it didn't come. With a whoosh it lost all its air and disappeared back into her mouth.

"Thanks," she said, giving me a skeptical look.

"I wanted to tell you on Friday, but I couldn't because there were a hundred kids surrounding you."

A little smile appeared and her perfect teeth glistened. "It was a pretty good race."

"Yeah."

"We'll make a good team, Josh and me," she said.

"Marwa will be great too," I said. "She'll probably bring really good ideas to the meetings."

"We'll see," Juliana said. But she didn't roll her eyes.

"It's pretty amazing that she won," I said. "I mean, she practically just got here."

"Yeah, well...weird things happen all the time," Juliana said.

The morning bell rang and we hurried in. We had never walked together before.

"Hey," Juliana said suddenly. "What the heck did toads have to do with anything anyway?"

I turned a deep, hot red. I had hoped that everyone had forgotten my slip. "Um...it just slipped out," I said sheepishly. "You know how Mrs. Benson makes us practice enunciation during music? I'd practiced the words so often they just..."

I waited for her to say something mean but she only said, "Oh, so that's what happened! And you didn't let it bother you. Wow. I never would've been able to do my speech after that."

Juliana popped her gum again, but for some reason it didn't bother me quite so much anymore. I figured Baba's recipe was working.

We had just reached our lockers when I heard someone chanting.

"Here comes the loser! Make way for the loser!"

Austin! He was standing near the door, beating a pencil against a book like a drum. I looked at Juliana.

"I'm talking about you, loser!" he growled.

And then something strange happened. It was like I was a parakeet who had been locked in a cage forever and someone came along at last and opened the tiny door. I whirled around.

"Shut up!" I screamed at the top of my lungs. "You just shut up! I am not a loser!"

And then I pushed him so hard with both my hands that he fell back two whole steps.

"Wh...? Hey!" He threw out his arms, trying to catch his balance.

"Woo-hoo!" Juliana whooped. "Way to go!"

I jabbed my finger toward him. "Get lost!" I screamed again. "And never, never, *ever* call me that again!"

Juliana held her hand up for a high five and I slapped my palm against hers, hard.

I turned to Austin one more time and screamed, "Jerk!" I was hot all over but my heart wasn't hammering like it usually did. I wondered if being fearless felt a little like this.

Conversations

I'm going to do a three-panel display board with information about the basic beliefs and the five practices of Islam," I told Winnie that afternoon. "And also something about the moon, because the Islamic calendar is a lunar calendar."

"I'm wearing the *hanbok* dress my Korean grandmother sent me and I'm going to sing a song she taught me. It's called the *Santoki*," Winnie said. "It's about a little bunny that lives up in the mountains. My Halmunee taught me all the words in Korean. And I figured I'd bring our menorah for the Jewish part of me. And driedels too. I bet those will be a hit with the little kids."

"Sounds great! I'll recite an Urdu poem about a boy named Bhaee Bhuttoo," I said.

Our project was beginning to take good shape but I was worried about the white space that still showed on my display board.

"Ask Marwa," Winnie suggested. "I bet you anything she has a few more ideas cooking in her head."

"Oops, I forgot all about Arab contributions in math and science. It was Marwa's idea actually and I guess that should cover it," I said feeling a lot better. "And OCD says I should bring a prayer mat and wear the shalvar khameez outfit she gave me two years ago for Eid."

"That OCD is one weird lady," Winnie said.

"Actually, her idea's pretty good but doesn't she realize I'm a whole lot taller now?"

After Winnie left, I found Mom curled up on the sofa watching TV. Amma and my brother had gone to the dollar store and both Badi Amma and OCD were napping.

"Amma spoils Zayd too much," I grumbled. "He doesn't need any more junk. Do you know how cluttered his toy chest is already?"

"She did the same with you, or have you forgotten?" Mom smiled. "Don't be too surprised to find some of that junk in the time capsule she's putting together for you."

I was supposed to open Amma's time capsule on my sixteenth birthday. She was filling it with things that represented the milestones in my life.

"Winnie says her Halmunee could never think of such a cool idea—not in a zillion years," I said.

Mom nodded. "I've met Winnie's grandmother. She's a tough lady."

"Amma's not a tough lady," I said. "My grandmother is the best and the smartest and the most fun!"

I sat down with my mother and watched TV for a while. I hardly ever had her all to myself like this. It was nice. *And, I said to myself, it's the perfect time to talk about the idea that has been wiggling around in your mind lately.*

"I've been thinking, Mom," I said in a casual voice. "What would you say if I wore the hijab?"

Mom's eyes were still glued to the TV. "You mean during prayer? That's silly, you already do."

"No, I mean *all the time.*"

My mother looked over at me. "That's an interesting question."

"Well?"

"I don't know," she said. "It's kind of sudden, isn't it?"

"Everyone talks about it, Mom. You see them everywhere now."

"Yes, but what has that got to do with us?"

"I'm just asking what you might say."

"Where is this coming from, Aliya? It is Nafees?"

"Oh, Mom, not Nafees. You know she'd stop the minute she could. Her parents force her to wear the hijab."

"Is it Amal then? Or Marwa? And what about the incidents with Sehr and her sister? You still want to talk about the hijab?"

"It's none of them and none of that," I said. "I wish you'd just answer my question."

"Okay then..." Mom sat up and turned to face me. "This is what I'd say. I'd try to talk you out of it. I'd tell you to reconsider and repeat my take on it. The hijab is a symbol of modesty—a good symbol, but a figurative one. We are capable of maintaining a modest aspect in our lives in other ways. I thought you already knew my thinking on that."

"I do, Mom," I said. "But what if—"

"What if you were determined to wear it? I'd have to really pay close attention, wouldn't I? Perhaps you'd show me what I was missing. Because ultimately it is a religious injunction that I've chosen to disregard. Who am I to decide for someone else?"

"Thanks for talking with me about it, Mom," I said.

"It just surprises me to hear that you want to wear hijab," she said.

"I don't," I said. "It was just a what-if question. You don't need to jump to any conclusions."

The idea had entered my mind a few days earlier when I was standing in front of our hall mirror, draping the scarf around my head. I imagined myself at school, in the middle of four hundred kids. Wearing the hijab in the face of ridicule was no small thing. But Marwa did it.

Not so long ago, Marwa shared with me her father's views on her decision to wear the hijab: *It's easy to do what our heart tells us. It's a heck of a lot harder to obey our mind.* I understood those words a little better now, but Marwa was Marwa and I was Aliya. What worked for Marwa would probably not work for me. She wore the hijab with as much assurance and ease as if she were in the streets of Morocco or Lebanon. As for me...I don't think so.

"Are you sure it's just a what-if question?" Mom asked.

"Yes, it is," I answered. "Honest."

Khuda Hafiz, OCD

Saturday, January 12
6:30 p.m.

Dear Allah,

A ton of great fund-raising ideas keep rolling out from the student council. I told Winnie I knew exactly who was behind these ideas but she said we should ask Juliana to be sure. I told her I bet she'd take all the credit. "Let's ask anyway," she insisted, so we did.

"Well...I've made a recommendation too," Juliana said, avoiding the question. "It's called Save a Seal."

"What does that do?" I asked.

"It saves seals," she said, rolling her eyes. "Duh!"

Yours truly,

A

PS Don't get me wrong. I'm not saying seals aren't important. I'm just saying we should take care of poor people of the world first.

Just when we were finally getting used to having OCD around, she announced she was returning to Minnesota. Her bags were packed and waiting by the front door.

"Leaving already?" Badi Amma asked. "Stay, stay."

OCD grinned. "You tell us, 'Stay, stay,' but our daughter tells us, 'Come, come!'"

"I'm going to miss you, Choti Dahdi," I said. I had to admit that after two months I felt much less uncomfortable around her.

"Aii. Don't be so sad," she replied. "We will return soon, Insha' Allah! What are you packing for us to eat on the airplane, hanh?"

"It's a kebab roll, Great-Aunt," Mom answered.

"Halal?"

"Absolutely!" Mom said. It was a tuna kebab and fish was always halal.

OCD called Zayd and me to her. She pinched our chins and then kissed her fingertips. "Khuda Hafiz," she said. Then, pointing to both Zayd and me, she added in her own English, "You, you…two, two…very, very good childs."

We raised our hands to our foreheads for a final respectful goodbye and wished her Allah's protection. OCD followed Baba to the door, clutching her walking stick in one hand and the brown paper bag containing her halal fish roll in the other. Before stepping out, she turned and fixed me with a hard stare.

"Run!" she commanded me. "Run!"

"Do you want me to fetch something from your room, Choti Dahdi?" I asked, preparing to obey.

"*Nai, nai.* Run for *estoodent kunsul* next year, you hear?" she said, pointing her walking stick at me.

Oh.

"Insha' Allah, Choti Dahdi!" I told her. God Willing!

As she went out the door, OCD shouted, "Come see us in *Minnipolice!*"

Wednesday, March 6
9:00 p.m.

Dear Allah,

I'm helping with the textbook drive. When I told Sister Khan about it, she raised an eyebrow and said, "Ma'sha Allah!" She was not being sarcastic, though. Anyway, we collected a dozen textbooks at the Islamic Center for children in earthquake-affected parts of Pakistan. Marwa says that by the time we're done, we should have a good amount. I'm helping with the packing too. (I've started collecting boxes already.) I also volunteered to help with the Gift of Hope Drive. Our school's donating money from the school festival to buy fifty chicks for the women in African villages.

Yours truly,

A

PS I'm making Zayd pay ten cents for each food group from his plate that gets thrown away. (Mom's pretty happy with my efforts.)

PPS I'm going to suggest a T-shirt drive to help slum kids in Brazil. I found this idea on the internet.

PPPS My independent study project's due next week. I'm nervous!

Winnie and I set up our displays. I was so jittery, I kept bumping into things. I bit my thumbnail, trying to focus.

"Take it easy," Winnie said. "You're going to chew up your entire finger at this rate."

Winnie was dressed in her ceremonial hanbok and armed with a bunch of maps and dioramas. She set up her trifold board and neatly arranged her artifacts across from my display.

I tugged on my too-small shalvar khameez and spread out my prayer mat and prayer beads. My report was neatly presented in sections labeled Religion, Culture, and Traditions. Bollywood music played quietly. "I'm just afraid I won't be able to answer the tough questions," I said.

"What sort of questions?"

"Like, 'Why do you hate America?' and, 'Will you go to heaven after you kill the infidel?'"

"Do you?"

"Do I what?"

"Do you hate America?"

"Are you crazy? Of course not!"

"Fine. Tell them that and if you don't know the answer to other questions, just tell them that too."

Kids from the lower grades started coming into the room, so I pulled my scarf from my pocket and put it on my head. I took a deep breath.

I needn't have worried so much. The little kids stared at my shalvar khameez outfit and at Winnie's hanbok. They were polite and asked easy questions. Only once did I have to tell someone to write his question down so I could find the answer and get back to him.

Marwa's class came by later. She stopped in front of our displays and looked at everything carefully.

My scarf kept slipping off my head. "This is so frustrating!" I grumbled. I eyed her hijab, which always seemed to stay in place. "I can never seem to keep this thing on."

"I can show you, if you like," she said.

"Know something?" I said. "If I had known how, I would have added a hijab tying demonstration to my project."

Out of the corner of my eye, I caught a glimpse of Austin standing in front of Juliana's display. He seemed fascinated by the mirror box that was part of her project on learning disabilities. It was supposed to show people the difficulties LD kids faced with schoolwork.

Marwa looked over in his direction. "He has dyslexia, you know," she said. "He told me he's just been diagnosed."

"You're kidding! He's been so mean to you. Why would he all of a sudden go and tell you something so private?"

She shrugged. "Who knows?"

"I don't get it," I said.

"Neither do I, but I'm not complaining."

"Just look at him shooting daggers at me," I whispered. "He's probably thinking I'm a circus freak."

Austin stared so hard in my direction that I had to look away. Then he turned back to the mirror box.

"Hmm. He's being awfully quiet over there. Did you bribe him or something?" I asked.

Her eyes angled away for a moment. "I...don't know," she said slowly. "My father told me to talk to his 'good side' first. He said that if that didn't work, we'd definitely get the principal involved."

"Austin has a good side?"

Marwa giggled. "That's how I felt, but Dad said everyone has a good side."

I didn't think anyone cared if Austin had a good side. His bad side was enough to keep most people away. "What did you do?" I asked.

"Nothing special. I told him I'd like to be his friend."

"That's it?"

"That's it," she said.

"And?"

"And he's been pretty decent since," she said.

This was a little too much to take in all at once. Could I get Austin off my back by saying something nice? The trouble was, I couldn't think of anything nice to say to him.

Several kids had gathered in front of my project. "*Aa-ee-ay, thushreef la-ee-ay,*" I said in Urdu, just the way Badi Amma had taught me. The words meant, "Oh, come. Please do come! You are welcome!"

A couple of days later, Marwa thrust a small packet in my hand as we were leaving the cafeteria. "Open it," she said.

I tore the paper apart and a square cloth, the color of a pink rosebud, slipped out. Marwa caught it before it hit the ground.

"Ready for Hijab 101?" she said. Before I could reply, she had formed the soft square into a neat triangle and draped it around my head with an expert flourish. "Hold still," she commanded, and she proceeded to drape and pleat and pin and wrap and knot it. "There!" She stepped back to examine her handiwork.

"How do I look?" I fingered the soft beak at the forehead. Marwa made a circle with her thumb and index finger to show her approval. "You didn't have to spend your pocket money on me," I said. "You could have bought something for yourself."

"Don't be silly," she said. "It's a belated Eid present."

The hijab felt snug and secure. I'd tell Mom that the long Indian scarf was all wrong for prayers. We needed proper scarves and then we'd never have to worry about them slipping down our heads each time our foreheads touched the image of the Kaaba on our prayer mats.

"Thanks, Marwa," I said. "It's really sweet of you." I started to unfasten the safety pin since it was time to go back in, but then I stopped. Marwa was squinting at me.

"What's wrong? Do I look completely funny?" I asked in alarm.

Before I knew it, her fingers were gently tugging, tucking, and fluttering around my head all over again.

"You look perfectly fine," she smiled, her eyes following her fingers. "It just needed a little more tweaking."

"I really don't know how you do it…," I began, trying to hold still.

"What do you mean?" She took a step back to re-examine her work.

"Well, I've asked this before, but I really want to know. Are you ever embarrassed to wear this thing at school?"

Marwa shook her head. "Why should I be? I wear hijab on my head and I wear sneakers on my feet for PE. It's pretty simple."

"It's not the same thing," I said. "Nobody notices sneakers. But a hijab…it's way out there!"

Marwa nodded. "It's in everyone's face, right? But without it I'd probably feel the way you'd feel without sneakers for PE."

"But..."

"This is who I am, Aliya," Marwa went on. "And I am okay with it. Really."

She sounded so sure. She looked so sure.

"I wish I could think like you," I said.

Marwa smiled. "Just be you. This suits you and it's not going to slip off either. Go ahead and test it out. Shake your head really hard."

I shook my head till I was dizzy but the hijab didn't budge an inch. I went over the steps of Hijab 101 again: *form a triangle...drape...pleat...pin...wrap...knot.*

"It's pretty easy once you get the hang of it," Marwa reassured me. "I can show you the trendier ways later, if you like."

As we walked back to the building, we passed two kids from Marwa's homeroom. "Hey, we were watching you two back there," one of them said. "You look exactly alike."

Marwa and I looked at each other and smiled. "Thanks," we said at the same time, and then we both laughed.

Friday, March 21
10:00 p.m.

Dear Allah,

My feelings are pretty mixed up right now. Marwa and Austin are getting along, but he still hates me. What works for Marwa doesn't seem to work for me.

Except for the scarf...or should I say hijab? It stayed on just like hers does. Winnie, Leah, and Madison thought I looked cute so I kept it on. When Juliana rolled her eyes, I rolled mine right back.

I've been thinking… I told Marwa people don't notice sneakers like they notice the hijab, but that's not really true. Mr. Forbes, our PE teacher, notices right away! So I guess what I'm saying is people notice, one way or the other.

I paid Marwa a compliment today. I thought she'd be happy I wanted to be like her. But guess what? She just waved her hand and said, "Oh, just be you."

Yours truly,

A

PS I tried smiling at Austin a couple of times today but he ignored me. I don't know what else to do. Maybe tomorrow I'll try complimenting him about his bike or something.

PPS On a happier note, I think Winnie and I are getting an A on our project!

PPPS Sister Khan's Steps to Success project is due in a couple of weeks. I'm going to hand in this notebook, along with a paragraph explaining everything. But first I'll sit down and think carefully about what to say.

PPPPS What's in our head can do more harm than what's on it. (I'm writing this again so I don't forget).

Farewell

Zayd and I were watching TV, but I couldn't pay attention. I kept listening for the phone; I'd been waiting for hours for Nafees to call. Earlier at the Islamic Center she'd promised to fill me in on the latest news about Damien. When the phone finally rang, I jumped off the sofa and ran to pick it up.

"Tell me everything, Nafees," I commanded. "Right now!"

"It's not Nafees. It's me, Marwa."

I was really surprised. Marwa was the last person I expected to call.

"Hey, Marwa. What's up?"

And Marwa told me. She was moving!

It took me a full ten seconds to grasp what she had said.

"What? Moving?" I sputtered. "When? Why?"

"As soon as school's out. My father got a better job offer in Los Angeles. I wanted to tell you first."

"Thanks a lot," I said. "I'm glad you wanted to let me know first, but I'm not exactly jumping up and down with joy at the news. I'm really going to miss you!"

"I'm happy we got to be friends," she said after a pause. "I hope you can visit some day."

"Does Austin know?" I asked.

"I'll call him next."

"I bet he's going to be pretty mad you're leaving," I said. "He'll probably take it out on me!"

There was silence at the other end.

"Are you there?" I asked.

"Uh-huh."

"I wish you were staying," I said.

More silence.

"We'll e-mail each other, all right?" she said after a little while. "We'll still be friends."

"Yes, yes, yes!" I screamed in the receiver.

Sunday, April 5
9:30 p.m.

Dear Allah,

Marwa's moving to Los Angeles when school ends. She said she wanted me to be the first one to know. I don't mind telling You, I am pretty upset! We were getting to be real good friends and she was helping me in lots of ways. But guess what? I am not going to wallow. I'm going to be happy for her and wish her a good life in California.

Yours truly,

A

PS Badi Amma says the hardest arithmetic to master is the one that allows us to count our own blessings. Well, I've been feeling pretty blessed lately and here's why:

- Marwa came! And she became my friend.
- I told Austin I bet he was the best biker in the whole school. "No kidding!" he snorted, but he didn't call me Alien.
- Amma tells me I've planted my own mango seed and my garden will bloom as long as I keep it watered. I think "mango" and "water" are metaphors. We studied about those in English.
- I don't feel like such a fraidy cat anymore! Al humdu lillah!

I read the letter over. It sounded like a pretty good conclusion. I flipped back to the beginning of my notebook and proofread all my letters for spelling and punctuation mistakes. It was a decent collection; I felt pretty confident that this was what Sister Khan had in mind. Now there was only one thing that remained. I gathered some thoughts together, turned on my laptop, and typed up an introductory statement.

Steps to Success
Religion 2: Sister Khan
Submitted by Aliya S.

For this project, I wrote letters to Allah. I am submitting twenty letters. I started writing before Ramadan began and I kept going.

Writing the letters helped me a lot. At first, I just wrote them because it helped to put my feelings down, but later I began to do more. My mother would say that at some point, I began to climb out of the hole. I didn't understand at first, but I understand better now.

I understand a lot of things a lot better now.

I hope that you will approve of my project. I worked really hard at it and I think I improved.

> *Respectfully submitted,*
> *Aliya*

My project was done. I picked up the notebook and went downstairs to show Badi Amma.

Extra Credits

On Monday, Mrs. Doyle came up with another one of her impossible assignments. This time it was an extra-credit writing challenge. Thinking about it was driving me bananas, but Winnie was her usual cool self. A week passed before I finally convinced her that we needed to give the project our undivided attention. We agreed to meet at her house.

We had our work cut out for us. There were a ton of vocabulary words; we had to put them all together in a good story that made sense.

Winnie made us both some lemonade and we carried it up to her room.

"How are we going to put thorps, tresses, coot, and audacious in the same story?" I asked. We had other words like indefatigable, delirious, befuddled, anatomy, propel, curmudgeon, slovenly, and vivacious to worry about too.

Winnie pondered the question for a moment. "We could make up a story about a befuddled old curmudgeon named OCD who lives in a propel thorp in Minneapolis with a slovenly grandniece named Alien whose anatomy consists of long, dark tresses and who has an audacious coot named Zayd for a pet."

"Ha, ha…very funny!" I said. "There is no such thing as a propel thorp and Alien doesn't have to be slovenly. She could be vivacious."

"Picky, picky!" Winnie said.

"And besides, what about indefatigable and delirious and doldrums and the zillion other words?"

"You worry too much," Winnie said, crunching ice between her teeth.

"Nuh-uh." I sipped my lemonade. It felt cold on my tongue. "I'm mostly wondering." Actually I was a teeny bit worried. I couldn't help it. But I felt like things would be okay. We'd pull it off somehow, just like we had with the independent study project.

I tipped my glass up to my mouth and the ice hit my teeth. I took another big gulp of my lemonade and swished it around in my mouth. The icy sweetness coursed down my throat and cooled me off.

No, I wasn't exactly worried.

Winnie and I were good partners…we'd figure out indefatigable and delirious and bravado sooner or later. We'd get it all done in good time.

"It's about time, Aliya," Zayd growled. "Where were you anyway? In China?"

"Apa!" Amma reminded him from the sink. "She's Aliya Apa. Why do you have to be reminded a hundred times in a day?"

I ignored my brother and plopped down on the sofa. I closed my eyes and let my thoughts float freely. I found myself thinking about Marwa. Before she moved away, I'd invite her to walk the spongy trails that wound around the lake through the trees. Together we'd look for wild mushrooms and rabbits; we might even spot a deer if we got lucky. Later, we'd dip our toes in the cool water and run our fingers through the oatmeal-colored sand. We'd eat the samosas that Amma would insist we take along.

I'd invite her first thing at school on Monday.

I stretched my legs out on the couch and watched images changing rapidly on the TV screen. My brother lay sprawled on the rug with his chin cupped in his palms. "I'm going to my room," I called to my grandmother.

The scent of OCD's rose-petal attar still lingered, but the room didn't ring with crazy cries of "Aii! Tauba, tauba!" I lay down on my bed and stared at the tulle canopy, ruffled and frothy. I closed my eyes and lay as still as the American Girl doll that stood on my shelf.

After a while, I got up. I rummaged in my drawer for Marwa's gift, the pink hijab that went perfectly with so many of my clothes. I tied it on, just the way she had showed me.

Step one: form a triangle. Step two: drape. Step three: pleat.
Step four: pin. Step five: wrap. Step six: knot.

I patted my head and stared at the girl in the mirror.

I stared and I stared and she smiled back at me.

Words and Phrases in Arabic

Aliya and her family are Muslims. Arabic is the language in which the Koran, the Muslim holy book, is written, and Muslims use many Arabic words both in their religious practice and in their daily life. Translations of words used in the text appear below.

Abbayah: A long, loose gown worn over clothing, intended to hide the curves of a woman's body
Adan: The call to prayer
Al humdu lillah: Praise be to Allah
Allah: The Muslim name for God
Allahu Akbar: God is great
Ameen: Amen
Assalam alaikum: Peace be upon you
Bismillah: In the name of Allah
Eid: Islamic celebration of either one of two events—completion of Ramadan or the completion of the pilgrimage to the Kaaba in Mecca

Eid Mubrook: An Eid greeting equivalent to Happy Eid

Halal: Meat slaughtered in the prescribed manner, with the name of God spoken at the time of the kill

Hijab: A scarf worn to cover the hair on the head

Iftar: A light meal eaten to break the Ramadan fast at sunset

Imaan: Belief; faith

Imam: A person qualified to lead the congregation in prayer

Insha' Allah: God willing

Kaaba: The first house of worship in Mecca, believed to have been built by Prophet Abraham

La hol walla: There is no power except God Almighty

Ma'sha Allah: As God has willed; used as an expression of wonderment and compliment

Makah Sharif: Revered Mecca

Mecca: A city in Saudi Arabia; the birthplace of Prophet Muhammad

Ramadan: The month during which Muslims observe a thirty-day fast

Ramadan Mubrook: Happy Ramadan

Suhur: The pre-dawn meal eaten before the Ramadan fast

Wa lil lahil hamd: All praises and thanks are for Him

Wudu: The Islamic procedure for washing parts of the body using water, typically in preparation for formal prayers

❁

𝔚ords and 𝔓hrases in 𝔘rdu

Aliya and her family use words and phrases in Urdu, the language spoken by most Muslims in India and Pakistan. Urdu is written right to left, in a modified version of the Persian alphabet, which is itself a derivative of the Arabic alphabet. Translations of words used in the text appear below.

Aa-ee-ay, thushreef la-ee-ay: Oh, come. Please do come! You are welcome!

Aap theek hain: Are you all right?

Accha: Okay; all right

Acchi bacchi: Good girl

Adab: A respectful greeting used by Muslims in the Indian subcontinent, performed by raising a cupped right hand to one's forehead

Ai hai!: Oh dear, o woe is me!

Aii: An exclamation of surprise, disapproval, disbelief

Amma: commonly used term for mother

Apa: Elder sister

Arre arre: Oh, what a shame.

Baba: Father

Badi Amma: Big mother (literal translation)

Baghare baigan: Heavily spiced eggplant curry dish

Biryani: Highly seasoned, aromatic rice with meat or vegetables

Budmash: Naughty, bad

Chaat: A savory snack typically made with chickpeas, potatoes, and tamarind sauce

Chacha: Paternal uncle

Choti Dahdi: Small paternal grandmother (literal translation)

Chup chaap: Silent, quiet

Churidar: Long, tight-fitting trousers worn by Indian men and women, worn with a kurta (a long, tunic like shirt) or a khameez

Dua: A prayer said for a specific purpose, not requiring a prayer mat

Dusterkhan: A long and narrow cloth, spread on the floor and used as a tablecloth.

Dhal: Lentil; spiced lentil curry

Dupatta: Long scarf, worn over the bosom and shoulders, which may be draped over the head

Eid Mubarak: An Eid greeting equivalent to Happy Eid

Eidi: A small monetary Eid gift for children

Hanh: Yes

Juldi: Quickly

Khala: Maternal aunt

Khameez: A long tunic with side seams left open below the waistline

Khorma: A type of curry dish made with meat, poultry, or vegetables, and seasoned with spices, nuts and seed pastes in a yogurt base

Khuda Hafiz: May God protect you

Kut: A heavily seasoned thick tomato sauce

Kya: What?
Kya bole?: What did you say?
Lumbu: Tall person
Mai abhi ayee: I just got here
Mamu: Maternal uncle
Meri Jaan: An endearment that means "My life"
Nai: No
Phupu: Paternal aunt
Pulao: Rice flavored with spices and cooked in stock, to
    which meat or vegetables may be added
Roti: Unleavened bread
Sari: A garment consisting of a length of cotton or silk,
    elaborately draped around the body, traditionally worn
    by women from the Indian subcontinent
Shaan Charga: A brand of spices
Shabaash: Well done
Shalvar: Baggy pants
Sheer khorma: A traditional Eid dessert, made with fine
    vermicelli, milk, sugar, nuts, raisins and dates
Shervani: A long, coatlike formal garment made with
    heavy suiting fabric
Tauba: For shame
Tum kub aye: When did you come?
Ujjad: Bad, awful, horrible

Farhana Zia grew up in Hyderabad, India. She is an elementary school teacher and the author of picture books and novels, including *Hot, Hot Roti for Dada-Ji* and *Child of Spring*. *The Garden of My Imaan* was inspired by a visit to her nephew's home in Illinois, where multigenerational family members coexist beautifully and enrich each other's lives every day. Her stories blend humor and tradition, memories and contemporary moments. Ms. Zia lives in Massachusetts.

www.fziastories.com